FARLEY'S JEWEL

A Novel
in Search
of Being

Jon
Ferguson

Farley's Jewel

CINCO PUNTOS PRESS   EL PASO, TEXAS

Brief passages in *Farley's Jewel* are taken from:
Heidegger, Martin. *Being and Time.* Harper & Row, 1962.
Nietzsche, Friedrich. *A Nietzsche Reader*, translated by R. J.
   Hollingdale. Penguin, 1977.

FIRST EDITION

Library of Congress Cataloging-in-Publication Data

Ferguson, Jon.
   Farley's jewel : a novel in search of being / by Jon Ferguson. – 1st ed.
   p. cm.
   ISBN 0-938317-34-2 (pbk.)
   I. Title.
   PS3556.E715F3 1998
   813'.54—dc21
                                        98-11948
                                           CIP

*Cover image from a photograph, "Self-Portrait," by Bruce Berman
Copyright © 1998 by Bruce Berman. Thanks, Bruce!*

Cover design by Vicki Trego Hill of El Paso, Texas.

Printed in Canada

For Francine

❧

With thanks to
Rus Bradburd & Steve Yellen
for their constant encouragement

PART I

WHILE FARLEY'S DOG was vomiting small pillows of white bile onto the vet's shiny tile floor, he—Farley—imagined he'd do his best to miss his own funeral. The dog had pulled a chicken carcass from the cold stove the evening before and had stood inanimate next to the living room sofa for an hour after Farley had come home. A bone was likely lodged in the stomach, the vet said. He had given the animal an injection to provoke vomiting and didn't seem to mind if the action occurred on his waiting room floor.

"Good doggie, Freda," Farley said as he got up to ask the secretary for more paper towels. Freda glanced helplessly at Farley and resumed her heaving. Another foamy puddle fell under her nose.

"Good dog. Atta girl," Farley whispered when he returned and knelt with fingers widespread on a fresh towel. "God helps her who helps herself. Right, girl?" This time Freda dry-heaved.

The vet came into the room with an old woman in a grey overcoat and a brown dog. He bid them good-bye and shook hands with the woman. "How's the patient?" he asked, turning to Farley.

"She's thrown up at least twelve times. First yellow, then the white stuff."

"Good. The shot can also help produce a stool, so why don't you take her out back and if she does anything, bring it in and show me."

Farley took Freda to the parking lot. She walked laboriously toward a tub-size patch of grass. Farley watched her in the December dark dimly lit by the glow in the vet's office. Freda sniffed for a minute, then—to Farley's delight—squatted. She'll be all right, he told himself. He had more faith in his veterinarian than his own doctor, reasoning that a dog was somehow less complicated than a man. The dog's thigh muscles tightened and relaxed in rapid succession and Farley, squinting, thought he saw something peer through the anus.

Freda stood and ambled back to the blacktop. Farley went to the grass and sniffed where his dog had sniffed. He dropped to his knees, combed the grass with Kleenex and cold fingers, but found none of what he was looking for.

They went back inside empty-handed. It didn't matter, the vet said, and seeing a gentle upward twitch in the dog's ears, told them they might as well go home.

"Up, girl. Uppa, girl," Farley coaxed as the dog stood before the open rear door of his rented Toyota. "Up, girl. Just a little leap for Farley." Freda's ears hugged her head, her buttocks shook, she couldn't jump. "Up girl," he said again. When she didn't move, he reached round her midriff with both hands and lifted. Freda yelped death.

They headed home between trees and houses alive with the bulbs of Christmas. *Home* in this case was the vet's word, not Farley's. He was living in a two-room apartment just off Lafayette Boulevard on Peter Street since his wife gave him the boot and he had grabbed it. "Six months!" she had shouted, "I want you outta here for at least six months!" At the time Farley thought it was a good idea, but after the first day in his new quarters he'd changed his mind. His wife kept it all, except the dog which Farley had originally imagined would be sufficient company.

Since he moved in with the other nomads on Peter Street, his love for Freda had suffered. When he lived at home with his wife and kids, Freda had been Farley's escape. He would walk her near the reservoir for an hour of peace and come home happier than when he had left. He would throw her sticks in the oak forest behind the house, watch her prance and pant, and think man and dog had it better than God and man. He would feed Freda and she would hurl her tail against his leg. But now, since they had moved out, none of these former pleasures had the same inflated satisfaction. Walking around the reservoir was now an extension of Farley's imposed unpleasant solitude. Throwing and chasing sticks seemed an absurd example of how beings struggle to fill the empty tube that is time. Feeding the dog made Farley feel less like a giver of pleasure than a jailer passing slop through tight metal bars. And, in all likelihood, the dog was feeling the same relational strain.

Farley reached his hand between the bucket seats and felt for Freda's head. Her ears were still glued to her head. He rubbed her skull. The Toyota hummed past the Sizzler and Foster's Freeze. Farley's hand felt heavy on his pet's head. It had been a week since he moved out. In that time all his actions had held the same heaviness he now sensed in his hand. Washing the dishes after dinner had felt that way. Combing his hair in the morning. Turning on the radio. Carrying his coffee cup to a foreign sofa. Twisting the corkscrew to get at the contents of a bottle of California Pinot. Even lowering his body into his rented bed had been an act in which his members surrendered to gravity with a force he was unaccustomed to. Take a man out of his routine, he thought, and God's grace disappears. The world becomes a burden.

He put his hand back on the steering wheel. Freda groaned as if tired or nearing hunger. Was the bone dislodging? Farley imagined the dog's stomach, hitherto the recipient of crushed grains and horsemeat, now flattened like his son's punctured bicycle tire.

He turned into Peter Street and found a parking place on the road behind the apartment building. *Home* was not having to search to park the car. In Moraga, Farley had a double garage that opened when he pushed a gadget he kept in the glove compartment. Half the garage was for his lawn mower, his son's bike, his daughter's tricycle, his golf clubs, and an easel on which he sometimes painted abstract pictures. The other half housed the Volvo wagon, now driven solely by his wife.

Farley opened the door for Freda, but the dog stared at him. He pulled her collar and watched her stumble to the ground. To his surprise she made not a sound and took what appeared to be a couple normal steps.

"That's my girl," Farley said. "A little chicken bone can't get the best of my Freedie." The dog stopped, waited for her master, then followed his slow pace to the apartment entrance. The concierge had put a small plastic Christmas tree atop the mailboxes, adorning it with silver tinsel strands and miniature colored lights.

"Merry Christmas," Farley mumbled.

They mounted the stairs to the first floor to a door that had the number 8 on it.

"Home sweet home," the master said. They entered, Farley fingering the wall for the light. He turned on the living room light and went to the refrigerator for a beer that he half drunk before he got to the couch. The can felt heavy. He felt heavy as he sunk into the phony leather black cushion. The air in the apartment smelled different than his home in Moraga, an odor of spice—like incense— a residue of previous renters. Freda came to him and managed to get her front paws onto the sofa. Her eyes glowed into his chest. He finished his beer, then went to the kitchen to feed her. The kitchen was an open rectangle attached to the living room. He took a plate from the cupboard, opened a large can of Alpo, heaped the contents onto the plate. Standing over the food Freda half-raised her ears. She looked up at Farley and began to eat.

"Good girl," Farley said. "The ol' bone must be on its way out." He imagined a needle free-floating in a balloon.

The dog ate three-quarters of her meal, sauntered to the couch and made it up. "Good girl." Freda curled up against him. He was on his second beer.

$\backsim$

T HAT NIGHT as he tried to fall asleep Farley wondered how a man could miss his own funeral. Why he had had the idea while Freda was throwing up on the veterinarian's floor, he didn't know. You die, they gather you up, say a few words and put you under. If in dying, he thought, there's nothing left of *you*, you miss the funeral that can no longer be for you. But if you're not there to miss it, the thing falls through.

Farley fell asleep but woke at three in the morning. When this happened at home he would go into the kitchen, smoke a cigarette, crawl back in bed next to Carole, and within minutes regain his prior state. Here it was different. There was no place to sit in the kitchen so he went to the sofa. He had two cigarettes then went to the window and stared at the cars parked along Peter Street. The bed failed to beckon. He thought of going out for an early breakfast, but didn't. He poured himself a glass of Pinot from last night's bottle and lit another cigarette. Freda, stirring in her corner on the couch, grunted. Farley wished the dog had chosen to sleep on the bed with him, but she had preferred the couch from the first night. She would have been better than nothing.

Why, he asked himself, were blankets and sheets nothing? Maybe this was why she had thrown him out—for asking questions like that.

He had taken a sabbatical year for study, not travel. He told the school he was going to work on fitting Heidegger's notion of Dasein into a computer model. But he had begun to lose interest, both in the computer and Heidegger. What held him presently was the question of why water, when it drops over a fall, is white. One day while walking around the reservoir with Freda, he had watched the water being run off—it was clear until it fell into a thin canal; then it was white.

He didn't really care if the department would consider his work nonsense. As far as he was concerned, it involved questions equal to Heidegger's Dasein. What is water? What is white? Do objects possess color or is it the other way around? Does matter in motion change color? Does matter really move? Does matter be? He corrected himself—is there matter?

He still couldn't sleep. Freda was asleep. Carole would be asleep. So would the kids. He lit another cigarette, then waited for the earth to turn morning.

FARLEY PARKED the Toyota in front of the carless side of the garage. The children had gone to school an hour ago. He knocked once at the laundry room door and walked in.

"I told you to call before you come. And don't be walking in to somebody else's house. You don't live here anymore, you know." Carole was slicing a banana on a bowl of granola.

"Sometimes I forget," Farley said. "I was just on my way to the library."

"Stop forgetting and go the hell to the library," she grunted. Farley got a profile of the nose he loved more after a couple days absence. The only other place he'd seen the nose was on a white patio statue exhibited with garden furniture on a summer clearance at Sears six years earlier. He remembered because his daughter had been born three days before, in September, and he had wanted to have something new in the house when Carole came home with the baby. He had not bought the statue, likely imitated from Greece via the Louvre, because he didn't like the idea of another head on his wife's nose. That the head was a dead head or a head from somebody's dead imagination didn't matter. Instead he bought a ping-pong table.

"I just wanted to pick up my golf clubs," said Farley.

"Since when do you play golf in December? Got a foursome with Jack Frost and the Abominable Snowman?" Farley raised his left hand to eye level and with his thumb and forefinger sculpted the nose pointed at the cereal bowl.

"I thought I might play nine and try to forget what it is to get thrown out of the house for talking to somebody."

"Except for you, talking to somebody til two o'clock in the morning means that a week later you'll be sipping champagne on a sheepskin rug in front of a goddamn fire place." She was spitting granola buds. "I know you, Farley."

She knew him, she thought, but she didn't. It could have meant the champagne, but there was no necessary connection between talking to a former student until two and skipping out on your wife. My wife, he thought.

"Has she hit puberty yet, Farley?" his wife barked.

"I told you the girl is twenty-one."

"Old enough to sip champagne. Good for her. Better for you. When are you gonna grow up, Farley?" Now she was looking at him. During the winter months her nose inflated a bit in the middle. Actually he wasn't sure if it was an optical phenomenon stemming from the skin color change from summer to winter or if it had to do with possible mucous defenses the nose activated to fight the cold. Her profile, however, never changed. She chewed and swallowed and sipped coffee.

"I know what I want now, Farley, and it's not a forty-year-old man that needs to shoot BBs at baby chickens every two years."

"I didn't shoot this time and I didn't shoot two years ago." Farley walked to the table and picked up the sports page of the newspaper. "How'd the Warriors do last night? I don't have a TV, you know."

"Can't you read anymore? Heart beatin' too fast for the ol' brain, Farley?" Carole was past the rage stage and was now calculating coldness. For this, her husband was happy. The rage had lasted three days. She had done nothing but glare, strut, exhale noisily, and repeat "You're outta here for at least six months!"

He had gone on the fourth day, thinking maybe it wasn't a bad idea after all. He'd been through such scenes a hundred times in eight years, the first on the plane to Europe for their honeymoon. Carole thought Farley had eyed the stewardess, firm and flowery in her Air France uniform, as she bent near his shoulder to refill his coffee cup. He had seen her, he explained, like he had seen millions of meaningless others. But Carole didn't buy his psychology.

Paris had not been shared. She had raced in front of him up the Champs Elysée, hidden in the corridors of the Louvre, and left him alone to drink a bottle of Chateau de Panigon in the Restaurant du Quai while she ran across a bridge to the Ile St. Louis and pondered a leap in the murky Seine.

Geneva had been better. It was raining and they stayed in their room for two days, the only possible source of conflict being the room service deliverer who, by heavenly benediction, was a male. Venice was a return to hell. The hotel clerk was an almond-eyed Florentine with mahogany hair and skin like soft lettuce. Farley had made the mistake of practicing his tenth-grade Italian on her. Husband and wife henceforth took separate vaporettos, fed different families of pigeons in the Piazza San Marco, and experienced coital joy only once in five days and four nights. Their honeymoon was over, though they flew home more glued than when they had left: Carole was pregnant with Ricky.

Farley put down the newspaper and started for the door.

"Where's the dog? You leave your second mistress in the penthouse?"

"It's no penthouse, Carole, she isn't a mistress, and Freda's in the car."

"Since when can you take dogs on the golf course?"

"I don't know what I'll do with her. You want her?"

"I told you she's yours. You're the one who has the dogs-aren't-animals-are-people-we're-all-built-of-the-same-stuff routine. She's your woman now. Take her. Go back and tend your kindergartner."

"She's twenty-one, Carole."

"And you're twelve. Out Farley!"

He left through the door to the garage, forgetting his golf bag.

He drove through the Berkeley hills to the Theological Seminary Library. He thought he'd give Heidegger another try, but Dasein or no Dasein, he was still out on his ear in a two-room cave sleeping far from the children he loved and a wife he missed, didn't, and did.

He re-read two chapters of *Being and Time*—"Being-In-the-World in General as the Basic State of Dasein" and "The Worldhood of the World"—before rescuing Freda for a pee. She pawed friskily behind him as they walked uphill to a cluster of eucalypti. He unhooked the leash. She ran, head skimming the ground, to an appropriate corner of earth. Her body arched, her eyes rolled back. Relieved, she dutifully sniffed the area, then returned to Farley who had seated himself on a protruding root. With behind swaying and ears pointed back like bee wings, she nestled her muzzle into his lap.

Never a more perfect face, Farley thought. Her mother was mostly Husky and her father Belgian Shepherd. Freda's amber eyes were set apart by a white stripe that ran down the middle of her beige and black snout. Her ears were triangular flames that rose and fell in accordance with her inner needs. Black lines round her eyes looked to have been stroked with a Chinese watercolor brush.

Farley rubbed under Freda's jaw, pondering how far back, mother to mother, she went. He saw, framed between igloo and tundra, a family portrait that crept back ad infinitum. For Freda to be, all her ancestors had to have been, to have been, to have been...

He sensed the infinite. Here there is no creation. Creation merely begs the question. Whatever was necessary to bring about the warmth in his lap has always been. Like ordering a milkshake, Farley thought—we're satisfied with its origin when we see the boy behind the counter scoop the ice cream into the silver container. That's as far back as we need to go. With dogs, we go to mother and father. With people, we hit a few layers of grandparents. With kings, we might dip into the Middle Ages.

Can't chew on infinity, he mused, lighting a cigarette.

Freda was returned to the Toyota and he to the library.

"When Dasein is resolute, it takes over authentically in its existence the fact that it *is* the null basis of its own nullity. We have conceived death existentially as what we have characterized as the possibility of the *im*possibility of existence—that is to say, as the utter nullity of Dasein. Death is not *added on* to Dasein at its 'end'; but Dasein, as care, is the thrown (that is, null) basis for its death. The nullity by which Dasein's Being is dominated primordially through and through, is revealed to Dasein itself in authentic Being-towards-death...When the call of conscience is understood, lostness in the 'they' is revealed. Resoluteness brings Dasein back to its ownmost potentiality-for-Being-its-Self. When one has an understanding of Being-towards-death—towards death as one's *ownmost* possibility—one's potentiality-for-Being becomes authentic and wholly transparent."

Farley shut the book, raised his nose and breathed. The place smelled like a coffin. Better free Freda before the funeral. Dogsein-in-the-Toyota needs a leak. Who reads Heidegger anyway? A-few-undead-Daseins-and-not-because-they-want-to. Most of them under twenty-five. He wouldn't teach 448 again. There were other ways to make a living. He'd teach a course on why water turned white when it dropped. Twenty-one-year olds with skin like the Italian receptionist would enroll. And they'd want to talk and sip expresso or rosé and admire the intelligence that he thought was something else. Carole hated the intelligence that she thought he thought he had. He thought it was something else.

He would leave the library and go to Peter Street with Freda. He would have a beer in one hand and the dog's head in the other. He would kiss the head. It would be warmer and hairier than a good breast.

Rᴵᴄᴋʏ UNSCREWED the peanut butter jar and dug in with three fingers. Rosanne shoved her way up to the table screaming for more than an equal share. "Daddy said I could have it!"

"He did not!"

"He did too!"

Ricky rapped Rosanne with a side-arm forearm. She fell from the chair—the peanut butter from the table—as Daddy rose from the toilet.

"Relax, kids. What's the problem?" Farley offered, coming back into the kitchen.

"She tried to take it while I was trying to eat it!" Ricky was howling too.

"But you said I could have it!"

"He did not!"

"Liar, liar, Ricky. Stupid!"

Farley hunted truth in family affairs like he did in the library—he was satisfied where there was none. "All right, kids, I got an idea. Why don't we have some ice cream?"

"Yayyyy!" they shouted in unison, racing for Daddy's refrigerator. "What kind you got?" Ricky asked.

"The swirly chocolate." Ricky was first on a chair and pulled the carton from the freezer.

"Ya got any bowze in your new house here, Daddy?" Rosanne asked.

"Got it all, kids. Got it all. They're in the cupboard above the sink." Rosanne mounted another chair.

"Ya only got two bowze here, Daddy."

"Just put mine on a plate."

"Whereda spoons?"

"In the drawer in the table."

"Ya got a scooper?"

"Just use a big spoon there. Okay. So tell ol' Popi what you kids want Santa to bring you."

"I already told ya, Daddy. I want a telescope and a Lego pirate boat."

"That's all?"

"Well, maybe one of those radar-controlled airplanes and a salamander."

"Now where's Santa going to find a salamander, Ricky?"

"Gimme a break, Daddy. You get 'em in the pet store at the mall."

"Santa has listened. What about you, Rosanne?"

"I wanna a eyephant an a yion an a...a..." The telephone rang.

"It's Mommy!" Ricky cried, running to answer in the living room. Freda knocked him down at the coffee table. Sobbing, he picked up the receiver. It was Mommy wanting to tell Daddy not to forget to give their daughter a suppository before bed. She'd been coughing for two nights. Farley asked for the phone. Before he said "Carole" she said, "I didn't call to rewrite the Declaration of Independence. Just don't forget to stick the suppository in the kid's ass and don't forget to put butter on it."

"On what?" Farley asked.

"The suppository, you brainless phallus!" His ear rang.

"What are you doing?" Farley asked gently.

"Screwing plumbers and French kissing mailmen. Don't forget to read the kids a book and kiss them goodnight if your lips aren't raw." She hung up, then called back to talk to Rosanne.

At nine-thirty the kids were asleep in Farley's bed. He fixed a salad, ate it with foreign cheese and a bottle of burgundy, then dropped into a makeshift bed on the couch and slowly found sleep.

It is Halloween. Farley is sitting on grass high on a mountain. The sun is down. Fading blue with ethereal stripes, the sky holds a velvet moon. Freda is wandering within sight of her master. The pines to Farley's right are yellow green and appear to have microscopic lamps in their needles. Across the valley the earth is red where earth is. Darkening red. Under him (under?), through his trousers, he feels the world cooling. His eyes roam, then settle on the rim of a peak across the valley. He senses motion there, a stirring speck like a struggling sperm. It enlarges. It is coming toward him as if on an invisible cable. When its form is clearly in view, Farley is not surprised that it is a woman. She is naked but for a mask and is carrying a brown paper bag. Trick or treat. Her breasts wobble up-down up-down, her hips grind a circle. Farley lies on his back awaiting her arrival.

The sky is now the blue before the black. She reaches him in the same now. She lingers suspended, then lowers her midpoint slowly to his face. He licks and sucks, his teeth and tongue levers and pullies, until she rises with a shriek of joy. Farley. O Farley. Face down (down?), she floats away. In leaving she removes her mask and Farley is not surprised that it is Carole. He is still dreaming when he tells her of his dream. But Carole does not believe him when he tells her she was the woman.

This, he thinks on awakening not unhappily on the couch, is the story of their eight years.

SEVENTY BUSINESSES are the Sun Valley Mall: nine shoe shops, a pet store, fifteen outlets for women's apparel, eleven for men, a TV and hi-fi seller, a drug store, a record shop, a Sears, a J.C. Penney, three movie theaters, a bookstore, a travel agency, one large toy store, Macys, a Gap, a stationary shop, eight restaurants, an ice cream stand, a frozen yogurt stand, a dry cleaners once owned by Farley's father, two jewelry stores, a sporting-goods distributer, a rental place for wedding attire, a luggage seller, a candy store, a cookie store, an imported comestible shop, and finally a store Farley didn't know what to call. The place he didn't know what to call had black walls and strange fluorescent lighting. The owners were peddling a variety of products like posters of oddly coiffured people, patches to be sewn on jackets (Farley thought), T-shirts—mainly black—combat-like boots, records with jackets promoting scenes of horror and gore, and an assortment of silvery heavy jewelry. In any case, the place was doing a good business in spite of having little that Santa Claus might deliver.

Farley had gone into the mall for the pirate ship, the telescope, the stuffed animals, and—perhaps—the salamander, but where do you hide a living gift? Initially it was his fellow men that had distracted him, but later it was the shops themselves. He had walked up and down both levels of the mammoth tube making a mental note of each commercial establishment. He paused longest before the dry cleaning shop that had originally belonged to his father, *homo mortem*. Farley Sr. had been an attorney and a good one. Unfortunately for the family finances, the practice of law had never quenched his money-making thirsts. He had had to invest, usually throwing his savings into ideas about which he knew nothing (tug-boats, soybeans, cancer cures, kiwi orchards) given to him by talkative and amiable clients. The dry cleaning scheme had been the brain child of a divorce customer who peddled the miracle machines that took spots out of clothes. The man was seeking celibacy at the same time the Sun Valley Mall was being built. One plus one stirred a vision in Farley Sr. that he couldn't kill: *Farley's Fleet Cleaning* beaming and beckoning just inside the middle upper-level entrance. His client pocketed forty-five thousand for the machines and solvents and he baled out twenty-two months later before his loss hit six figures. He sold the place to a couple from Fresno who knew the business. They first changed the name to *One Hour Dry Cleaner*, sold some unnecessary equipment, and cut out the "three-for-two" specials. Ten years later they were still there and likely doing very well. Farley watched them through the window. The man was steam pressing and the wife hanging garments and handling the register. Maybe, Farley pondered whimsically—trying to exculpate his adorable dead father—as civilization grows people spill more shit on their clothes.

Why had he made his count? he asked himself as he walked back to the toy store. Why had Freda eaten the chicken carcass? Why had Heidegger written *Being and Time*? Why did Rosanne want a stuffed elephant? Why had Carole thrown him out? Why does man have an urge to couple every three days or less? Why do we sully the brain with *why*? Why are we satisfied with one, maybe two *becauses*, when the becauses really go back as far as Freda's ancestors. Turn off the machine and play Santa Claus. Farley stepped into the toy store.

It was a year of Barbie and Ken, two-lane figure-8 roadrace sets, He-men, GI Joes, and an assortment of dinosaurian creatures built to destroy and be destroyed. The stuffed animals were in the back. The lions ranged from $7.99 for one the size of a baby kitten to $99.99 for one that would cover half of Rosanne's bed. Farley took a medium-size model that cost the equivalent of a steak dinner for two. Choosing the elephant was easier—there was only one sort.

What could you see through a toy store telescope? Your neighbors? A pine cone at mid-tree? He approached a clerk for its whereabouts. They were dressed in candy-cane shirts and were everywhere. The one nearest him had her back turned and was helping a grandfather choose a dinosaur. Farley waited behind her until she was free.

"Excuse me, but I can't find the telescopes." The girl turned and, when she saw Farley, blushed a shade of her shirt.

"Mr. Farley," she said coyly. "What are you doing here? I thought you were on sabbatical."

"I am, but I didn't go anywhere. How long have you been working here?" He wanted to call her by name but *Elizabeth* didn't come to him until she had begun to answer.

"I'm just doing the Christmas holidays to make a little money." She looked as good as she had in class, and always better when he and Carole were at war. Her hazel hair had been cut from shoulder-length to just below her delicate ears—silver earrings dangled from them.

"How is it," he inquired, trying not to sound professorial, "being surrounded by all these happy givers?"

"It's not bad really, but I'm not sure I'd want to make a career out of it. I always liked Christmas. I remember that time in class you told us that Christianity without Christmas would be like golf without balls."

"I did?"

"It was in your Contemporary Religions class. When was it...(she stares dreamily into Farley's black turtle-neck sweater) three years ago I guess."

"Are you still in school? I don't think I've seen you for at least two years. Last time was at the Safeway in Moraga. (He thinks longingly of his empty bed on Peter Street.) You remember?"

"You were buying watermelon."

"You remember." Farley remembers he's looking for the telescope. "Elizabeth, do you sell that children's telescope here?" (He is not trying to forget her, but she is afraid he is. Two lines later she is happy to see that he isn't.)

"Yeah, Mr. Farley, they're over next to the model airplanes."

"You don't have to call me Mr. Farley anymore."

"What should I call you then?"

"Farley. Just Farley's fine."

"Okay. Let me show you the telescopes." (She always knew where she was going, he thinks.)

"Sure." (What else can I show him? she wonders.)

She leads him to his son's desire and takes one out of the box. She sets it up on a stack of cartons. He kneels and stares through the aperture at the ceiling of the toy store. It is corrugated, white, grey with black specks. Farley thinks he could be looking at the moon and wishes he were. He rotates the telescope to where it is aimed at Elizabeth's face. She is a pinkish beige blur.

"Does the thing really work out there in space?" he asks.

"I wouldn't make any bets on finding Pluto, but I'm sure it does something. You're one to ask questions about space, Mr. Farley."

"Farley."

"Oh, sorry. You told us there wasn't any, remember?"

He has stood up and has pointed the wrong end of the telescope at her feet. He remembers how daintily they were always crossed farthest from the door on row one. He says, "Any what?"

"You said you had a vision or an inspiration or something once on a mountain and everything was one thick totality and that it was really only man that created space."

"I think you were a better student than I was teacher," he babbles into the lens he is now aiming at her nose. She advances putting her left eye to the small end. (She always knew where she was going, he thinks.)

"Can you see me?"

"Not well enough," he doesn't mean to say but does. (I better get back to work, she thinks but doesn't say.)

"How old is your son now?"

"Seven." They both pull back and he sets the telescope down on the carton. "Next year he'll probably want a microscope, so we might as well start with the big stuff. Can you wrap all this for me?" He hands her the lion and elephant and puts the telescope back in the box.

"Sure." (She can't get herself to say "Farley.")

"Oh, and I need a Lego pirate ship too."

As he follows her through the aisles of games, toys, trains, and plastic creatures, he feels a thrust of joy—joy unfelt of recent. There is something to the coming moment. At the Lego display, he asks her if she might want to go out for Mexican food after work. She wants to. They'll meet at El Charro in Lafayette at nine-thirty. Elizabeth wraps the gifts and bids Santa Claus good-bye.

Three years prior Elizabeth had taken two of Farley's classes during the autumn semester—Contemporary Religions and An

Introduction to Metaphysics. In both she sits first row, seat farthest from the door. As all good students do, she has chosen her classes for the teacher, not the subject. Bad teachers make everything a bore. Good ones can render a study of Medieval Veterinary Practices interesting. Elizabeth, however, has fit Farley into her schedule *pour le male, pas le maître*. Her freshman year she had been taking a class in French literature that was moved in mid-term to the philosophy building because of a fire in the French department. The class was stuffed into a small room next to Farley's office. He always left his door open—his walls of books had become bad scenery—and she passed by four times a week for two months. Her green nineteen-year-old eyes saw a man in shaggy sweaters and worn herringbone jackets with a Matisse charcoal nude behind his head. She wanted to be the nude when he, seen through the door, had his back to her as he sat slouched in his swivel chair. Charcoals don't breathe, she had thought. I do.

It is 10:10. The students are seated and Farley's loafers can be heard clopping through the hall. He enters Room 424, B Building for the first time this year. He throws a tattered briefcase on the desk and sits next to it. He speaks: to fifty-five open ears—the boy next to Elizabeth has lost one in a hunting accident: "Good morning. I hope you all had a nice California summer: sun, surf, sex, and sandwiches, right? Let's get started with me asking you a few indiscreet questions."

"Okay, who went to the beach this summer?" (12 hands)

"Who saw Clint Eastwood's latest film?" (15 hands)

"Who drove a car?" (27 hands)

"Who watched television at least three times during the month of August?" (28 hands)

"Who went to a bar?" (22 hands)

"Who ate at McDonald's at least once during the summer?" (25 hands)

"Who either heavily petted or copulated with a boyfriend or girlfriend?" (Slowly, then in a rush, 24 hands)

"Who played baseball, golf, tennis or ping-pong?" (26 hands in unison)

"Who read a book about metaphysics?" (Eyes look for other eyes. No hands, then one hand from the boy with one ear.)

"Who thought about metaphysical questions for more than half an hour during the months of July and August combined?" (Same one hand)

Farley looks at Elizabeth, then at the boy next to her and says, "What questions did you think about?"

The boy is not embarrassed, but is hesitant, "I...I often wonder if maybe God's thoughts are completely different from man's thoughts, then...then I start to wonder if there's any God at all."

"Thank you," Farley says. He stands up, ambles to the window near Elizabeth, then sits back down on the desk. As he does this Elizabeth's eyes climb his pant legs. "Has anybody here ever considered the possibility that space is an illusion, that is, that there is really no distance between objects and in fact the separation of objects is really nothing more than man's little dream?" (No hands, a lot of creases around noses and foreheads.)

"What do I mean?" he continues. "Let's make the idea simple. If in fact the entire universe is made up of matter—atoms, monads or something of the sort—then all this matter—it might be energy rather than matter—is all stuck together. That is, if the universe is all matter, then it is just that, ALL MATTER." (He pauses) "No holes, no space between one existing thing and another. Now we see the world all neatly divided...a desk here, a chair there...here a boy, there a girl (he gestures toward Elizabeth)...tree, ground, sky, cloud, etcetera. But maybe the way we see it all isn't really the way it is. Maybe, in fact, it's just our eyes, our consciousnesses, our brains, if you will, that make it look the way we see it."

The boy with one ear puts up a hand. Farley calls on him, but he thinks twice and says, "No, nothing. Maybe I'll ask you later."

"So if you get my point, isn't it possible that space—or shall we say distance between what we call *objects*—is really only man's way of seeing existence...man's way of defining and breaking down what might in fact be an unfathomable oneness of being?" Farley walks toward the window again and is a little taken by his speech. He does, for a moment, practice what he preaches, i.e. he feels a kind of unearthly lostness as he stares through the glass. This lasts until he glances down at Elizabeth who is chewing on her pencil. "What do you think about all this, mademoiselle?" he asks her sensing himself fall back to this world—man of tingling innards in presence of female beauty.

She blushes, (Does he know I had French class next to his office? Had he noticed me?) then says, "Well I...I never really thought about it before, but, but why not?"

"That's fine," the teacher says. "I don't suspect many of you have ever thought about it. I asked you about what you had done this summer simply to show you that we Americans, or Anglo-Europeans, don't bother with such thinking. We have words, numbers, newspapers, television, movies and the rest to create our ontological ground." The hand next to Elizabeth goes up again. "Yes," Farley says. "What was your name?"

"David Jorgensen, sir. I just wanted to know what ontological means?"

"Ontological. It's just a big word that refers to *being* or *reality*. When I say our ontological ground, I simply mean what we take to be real. Most of us never question what is real because we consider reality a given. A dog is a dog, right? But this year in our study of metaphysics, we'll see that maybe it's not all so simple and clear as we might otherwise think it is. We'll take our time and try to get ourselves to think and ask questions in ways that we haven't done before." Farley's use of *we* has his students relaxed and looking forward to seeing him again. The girl in front on the right will think of little else until their next lesson. After this lesson, she's next to last to leave the room. The boy with one ear has stayed to ask a couple questions.

Before going to El Charro, Farley took Freda for a run around the Lafayette reservoir. He ran too. Fellow joggers had told him it was a three-mile loop. When he ran, which was usually three times a week, his guiding principle was to run until it stopped feeling good. This could mean a half mile, more, less, but never had he gone around more than once.

Farley and Freda got to the reservoir at four-thirty. What sun the Bay Area hills had seen that day had since disappeared and now a steamy hoary fog perfused the pines and oaks. This was the air that had meant Christmas for Farley the boy and it still did. It smelt leathery. It smelled like wet rope. Walking from the parking lot to the trail, Farley paused to loosen his hamstrings. Freda was scurrying from tree to tree, her nose a Geiger tube searching the earth's sacred spots. Farley watched her with renewed affection. He whirled his arms twice in each direction then started to jog at a fox trotter's pace.

Freda ran in front of him, behind him, up the hill and down toward the water. Ten yards for him were forty for her. Farley crossed a fellow runner in the opposite direction and lifted his hand to evoke some notion of a shared existence, though the other was likely on his third mile whereas Farley was just warming up. Otherwise he met no one. Winter, he thought, is a bane for many a body. As he reached the first strenuous upgrade, he felt slightly tired but pushed to the top at a steady pace. On the downswing, his legs were light and his heartbeat echoed pleasantly in his skull. The fog had thickened which made running easier. The usual landmarks that announced how far he'd gone or might go were no longer visible. He sensed he was running only to be running instead of trying to get somewhere.

As he ran he pulled his wool gloves from his parka pocket and put them on. From the other pocket he took his knit cap. The cold was no longer felt. Freda had tired a bit and was now in a slow gallop beside him. Farley looked down and watched her front feet curl, then grip, the black asphalt. One two—one two—one two. When he raised his head he was on the second and last big hill. It seemed easier than the first. Over the top, he began to run faster and sensed his brain slow until it felt glued to the achromic funnel in front of him. Here, now, here, he thought, there is no death. His knees rose higher, pumping on the straightaway that was the dam. He looked left. The fog was sewn to the water without a stitch. He heard his feet. One-one-One-one-One-one-One-one-One-one-One. The funnel sucked him on, and on.

Farley and Freda did two loops. For the first and only time in his life, Farley was touched with the ecstasy that runners are known to gloat about. The ecstasy carried him for the last two miles, then back to the cave and home to Peter Street. It continued as he turned on the water in the bathtub and untabbed a beer. Ectasy ended with the ring of the phone.

"Hello."

"Where the hell have you been?"

"Shopping, running with Freda. I'm not quite sure why it should matter to you."

"I've tried to call you for three hours."

"I was counting the stores in the mall."

"You're hopeless, Farley."

"Aren't we all?" He took a thick sip of beer.

"My mother called and thinks we should all spend Christmas at their house. She says the separation is bad enough for the kids and that we should get the family together as much as possible during the holiday."

"Family means *your* family, right?"

"Farley, my family doesn't live in St. George, Utah. I didn't tell your father to move there. So do you want to do it or what? Or have you already got plans to drop through the chimney and show your gifts to one of your needy little cockamamie chippies? You always were such a great giver…"

"My father's dead and my bath water's calling."

"Well, turn it off and let's settle this. Christmas is for the kids and they happen to be *our* kids."

Farley turned off the water and returned, wondering why Christmas was for the kids. Was there a man alive who didn't like giving and taking? He swigged beer, then picked up the phone.

"I'm here."

"Is she?"

Is there no respite? Farley thought before saying, "Is there no respite?"

"Maybe. I don't know. Maybe Christmas will bring a fleet of angels to clean up the slime. Make that semen, or would you rather call it tinsel, given the season?" Farley knew his wife's invectives flew from a loving bow. So, in a sense, he didn't mind. Between man and woman what counts is that the other is there. The mode of being there is of secondary importance.

"Carole, when are you going to snap out of it?" he said.

"When you give me a reason to. Let's talk about Christmas." Her voice unexpectedly took on the tone of a dentist's—soothing, as when, syringe in hand, he says, *Now, can you open real wide for me*? "I think maybe my mother's right, Farley. You know what Christmas meant to you as a kid." She was into her telephone voice, the one that had seduced him eight years before when Carole, the daring graduate student, would call him in his office and rescue him from the mire of a Kantian or Schopenhaueruan brain. The vowels were long and meliferous, the sentences short and breathy.

"Listen Carole, I'm cold. I just walked in from the reservoir. I'll stop by in an hour and we'll talk about it."

She agreed and Farley took a fresh beer into the tub.

He got to the house at seven-thirty. El Charro was for nine-thirty. Carole was wearing a green cashmere sweater and her faded French jeans. A few locks dripped from her ponytail.

"Where are the kids?" he asked as they moved to the kitchen.

"They're already in bed. Last night we went through the Christmas catalogues again and they got so excited they didn't get to sleep 'til 10:30. Did you get them anything yet?"

"I picked up everything in the mall today. At least the big stuff."

"I got a few things for the stockings this morning," Carole said, her voice still tender. She inclined, thought Farley, to be either/or. My Kierkegaardian wife. Her face was a creaseless glow. He glanced at the calendar on the fridge, Xed out to the 22nd.

"So Santa comes in two days. I'd lost track," he said. "Okay, let's go to your parents. I see no reason to buck it."

"How about going up the afternoon of the twenty-fourth?"

"Fine."

"You want a drink?"

"A beer."

When she closed the refrigerater Farley intercepted her from behind and ran his hands up the cashmere. He nosed her neck and remembered one of the reasons he'd married her. In love she forgot everything and love could find a foothold most anywhere. The fridge clicked as they went to the floor. When the tinsel turned missile, Farley thought, Here there is no death.

MR. FARLEY, you remember you asked us to think about thinking? You said that historically the problem with metaphysics was—or is—that it should begin with thinking and if sense can be made of thinking then maybe we have a chance to get close to reality." The boy with one ear speaks with controlled nervousness while Elizabeth's eyes jump from him to Farley to him to Farley.

"Yes, David," Farley says.

"Well, the more I think about my own thinking, the more it becomes a mystery to me. I'm beginning to wonder if there's really an I that 'thinks' or if thinking is just something that happens to me or goes through me or whatever."

"You've done well to have taken it that far." The student smiles, rubs his hair, but is genuinely perplexed and intense. As Farley looks at the boy, he, the boy, begins to recede and melt into the colors and forms of the landscape to where his face is a pinkish dot. (Cezanne was right, Farley thinks. For the eye alone, the world is always a two-dimensional plane. For the eye alone, there is no depth.) Farley speaks again to try to bring the boy back into focus. "Have you been reading, David, or just thinking for yourself?"

"Actually, Mr. Farley, I've just been thinking. I can't see how reading somebody else can help me see my own thinking."

Farley looks at the class and says, "If you remember we said that in our world and everyday lives nothing seems clearer than thinking. Everybody constantly says *I think* this or *I think* that—'I think it's going to rain' or 'Don't you think that was a good idea?' or 'Go to your room and think about it' or 'The President thinks that the matter can wait' or 'You know what I think? I think you're full of shit.'" The students laugh and most hope Farley will change the subject but he doesn't. "But as David has found out, if we push things a little we see that what thinking is is not so apparent as we might imagine. Let's take a few minutes now and do what I suspect David has been doing. First, all of you tell yourself not to think. Try to turn off the machine, if you will. For the next thirty seconds don't think. Do you understand?...Okay...ready, go."

Elizabeth thinks that Farley's hair is marvelous, then thinks she can't stop thinking, then thinks: *All those half curls fighting for a place to dance on his head.*

David thinks that this is a good idea and thinks he knows where Farley is going to take the class.

Arthur Windell thinks, *I'm trying not to think, but that's thinking*, then is side-tracked to the A's game he's got a ticket for that evening.

Christine Lasenger thinks that she likes Mr. Farley, but maybe she should change her minor to anthropology or something. Then she thinks maybe she doesn't really know her father who suggested the philosophy minor.

Max Lippett thinks, *Whatthefuck, here goes*, but then finds his mind immediately full of a combination of thoughts and images ranging from Elizabeth's rear to Karl Marx's beard to words like STOP (He sees the word typed in capitals) and CAN'T and KANT and CUNT. Here the thirty seconds run out.

"Time's up," Farley says. The students exude relief. "Was anybody able to not think?" Max Lippett raises his hand.

"Yeah, well, I had a lot of images and stuff and maybe a couple words flashed through my head, but I'm not sure you'd call that thinking, would you?"

"Good question. Puts us back to what, in fact, is a thought?

What is thinking made of? Chemicals? Atoms? Matter? Spirit? Images? Words? Emotions? Numbers? Soul? Is is *made* of anything? And then we can ask, how are thoughts connected? Where does one begin and another end? Or is thinking a whole that cannot be subdivided? In our little thirty-second experiment I wanted you to see that maybe what comes into your head or consciousness is not really commanded by an I or an Ego or whatever you want to call it. Maybe we don't know where thinking comes from. If I can't tell myself not to think, maybe I can't tell myself to think either."

David Jorgensen raises his hand. Farley acknowledges him. "This might sound stupid, but the other night I woke up with a thought in my head that had nothing to do with anything. It was something like, like...'There's a spacing problem in the mall.' (Farley wants for a moment to believe in a some kind of para-communication, but knows he cannot. David goes on.) Now it seems to me that this thought just came to me. It's as if I don't think, but thinking thinks me, if you see what I mean."

"Yes, of course, David."

"I stayed up thinking about it for a while and it seems that the only reason this thought struck me funny is because it didn't fit into my normal thinking...I mean it still came to ME, so it's part of ME...but, well, what I'm trying to say is that maybe our normal thinking is really just as strange as stuff like 'There's a spacing problem in the mall,' but because it's normal, we don't bother to think about it. Maybe I'm not being too clear, Mr. Farley, but..."

"I think you're being very clear, David. It's just that we're dipping our toes in a pond that most of us aren't used to wading in."

The bell rings. Farley thanks the students for their participation and wishes them a pleasant weekend. He asks them to just once, during the weekend, stop and watch themselves thinking. Max Lippett fidgets at his desk trying to find a reason to exit last with David and Elizabeth. He won't think about his thinking, but will follow Elizabeth, his nose an iron bar and her ass an apodal magnet.

Farley watches the three float to the open door and thinks maybe it takes a lost ear to blow the circuit that is thinking.

$\mathcal{S}$

WHY DOESN'T America let dogs into its restaurants? A dog sleeping beside its master's feet makes more sense than a child spilling water glasses and throwing ketchuped french fries on the floor. If we ate them, Farley thought in the Toyota winding from Moraga to Lafayette, I could see it. No one wants a cow mooing next to his steak. But we don't...generally, he corrected. He didn't like to leave Freda in Peter Street, but a two-room apartment was better than a car, given that both auto and lodging were relative strangers. He adjusted his back in the bucket seat and felt some thigh hairs glued to his undershorts.

Farley got to El Charro at twenty to ten and found Elizabeth sitting in the waiting area under a petrified sombrero. The air smelled fried and peppered until he leaned to kiss Elizabeth's cheek which delivered the scent of a baby's skull.

"Sorry I'm late," he said taking her elbow.

"That's okay. I didn't get off 'til after nine. Christmas keeps those customers coming."

They were given a table behind the bar at the rear of the restaurant. The hostess lit a small vanilla candle in a frosted bowl and wished them a merry meal and a good Christmas. America, Farley thought.

Before they had finished their Margaritas and basket of taco chips, Farley felt the upper part of Elizabeth's leather boot push into his thigh. What is a man to do? he thought thinking of Carole and the flesh filtered through his partially deadened brain. He had run, bathed, had two beers, then his wife comfortably and considerately on the kitchen floor, and now Aphrodite was beckoning under the Mexican motifs of the table cloth. What was a man to do?

Elizabeth's jade eyes said nothing of her leg. She looked at Farley like she had looked at him in class, as if he were Moses yodeling the Sermon on the Mount and she his happiest sheep. Holy Farley, Aphrodite wants a sizable chunk of His Highness.

"Did you get all your shopping done?" she asks.

"Most of it, except the salamander."

"They've got them in the pet store in the mall."

"I know. I just didn't know what to do with it in the meantime." The same held for her leg. Would he push his, rub hers, pull his, or hold where they were? Yodel Moses, yodel. "Elizabeth, did I ever tell you what got me into philosophy?"

"No, I don't think so," she said, grinding her boot.

"You got a minute?" he asked. She answered with her eyelashes. "Actually, I had enrolled as a freshman in civil engineering, for what reason I really don't know. I suspect it was because my grandfather had been an engineer and I had thought him a good man. Anyway, Christmas of my freshman year my father had rented a cabin up in Tahoe. I don't remember exactly where, but there was a forest behind the place and I'd take our dog back there for walks." Elizabeth tried to picture Farley at eighteen. She saw a soft blond chest, a thin neck, lips curled out at the edges, a ski-jump nose, a rounded hairless jaw, and a head of sixties hair. Then she put an etching of lines under the eyes, gently sunken dimples, and a herringbone coat and there was today's Farley across the table.

"On Christmas day," he went on, "it started to snow and didn't stop for three days. There was so much snow we couldn't get the car out to go skiing. It was the day after Christmas—I remember because I was wearing a red parka my parents had given me the morning before—and I took a walk deep into the forest with the dog. The snow was light but steady. The sky was a grey blanket. I remember being so happy and thinking the world was so beautiful that I started to cry. I think I even kissed the trunk of a tree."

"Our dog was a wonderful bastard, some sort of cross between a Chihuahua and a German Shepard, but the thing was a hunter. As we walked the only sound you could hear was the crush of my boots on the snow. Suddenly the dog jumped into a clearing and I saw her muzzle flip a furry ball into the air. It was a squirrel. When it hit the snow I saw her jaw wrap round its head. I heard the muffled noise of the skull cracking. I didn't move for a few minutes while the dog jumped and whirled throwing the squirrel again and again in the heavy powder snow. The silence around me had changed from pristine perfection to a thick chamber of death."

Elizabeth pulled her leg, but only to adjust herself in her chair. It found Farley's corduroys as she said, "Here's our food. Please finish the story."

"That's really about it. You can imagine the rest. Boy looking tree-topward saying, 'So this is Your world.' Boy loving dog that loved to kill squirrels and who knows what keeps the squirrels alive. There was just the hard fact of innocent death that had me changing my major at the beginning of the second semester."

Elizabeth reached across the table and took hold of the baby finger that hung from the end of Farley's fork. Moses had yodeled well. What was a man to do?

CAROLE AND THE KIDS picked up Farley in the Volvo wagon at three o'clock the afternoon of the twenty-fourth. He and Freda were standing in front of the apartment when she pulled up. Beside him were three large garbage bags in which he'd hid Santa's surprises. Farley came round to the driver's side. Carole cranked a crack in the window.

"Do you want to see the penthouse?" he asked.

"Let's save it for your memoirs."

"Fine. Mind if I drive?"

"Sure," she said, surprising him. She climbed over the emergency brake while he tossed the bags in the back of the car. Carole had flattened the rear seat so Ricky, Rosanne and Freda had space for play, war, and sleep.

Carole's parents lived in the town of Paradise, three hours north of San Francisco in the California foothills. They had moved there from Los Angeles when Carole was ten and her brother Alvin nine to give the kids a shot at clean air, drugless adolescence, and language rooted in something other than beach, waves, woodies, wows, and hanging-tens. Her father had taught high school history and coached basketball. The athletic director at Paradise High was so impressed with his 2-2-1-full court press and his passing game that he went from frosh to J-V to varsity mentor in four short years. The fans liked his wild style, the players liked his pre-game speeches about Abraham Lincoln, Paul Revere, and Geronimo, and his boss liked the fact that his wins divided by losses produced the number 3. Carole's father liked Farley the first time he saw him play for Chico State eight miles down the road from his home.

Walt McOmber was now retired in a three-bedroom home tucked in the shadows of a family of towering redwoods just off Pentz Drive. Carole's mother had been retired since her son Alvin kissed her goodbye on the driveway and headed off for an institute of golf and higher learning in the Arizonian desert. Carole had already followed Farley to the Bay Area. Walt had another ten years of presses and passing games before he and his wife would share an equal social status.

The Volvo, a maroon bullet loping up the right lane past Martinez's oil refineries in the December twilight, suddenly veered off the freeway into a service station.

"I gotta go," Farley said. "Anybody care to join me?"

"Mommy, you said we could have some bubble gum," Ricky yelled.

"All right, come with me and we'll find the bubble gum," Farley offered.

"Carole, could you fill up the car?"

The kids followed Farley round the side of the station to toilets that were advertised as clean and were not. Ricky and Rosanne watched as Farley released a river of recycled coffee, orange juice and beer into the stained ceramic bowl to the rim of which clung 18 spider-leg curlicues by Farley's quick count. He zipped his corduroys and said, "Let's go find that gum."

"Daddy, didn't your mommy teach you to wash your hands after you go pipi?" Ricky asked seeing his father ignore the sink.

"My mommy taught me not to pipi on my hands."

"Come on, Daddy!"

"Come on, kids."

As Farley pulled the door to enter the service station Mini-

Market, a woman in cowboy boots, denim jacket and imperative bun-hugging jeans was on her way out. Farley held the door for her, she acknowledged him, and his neck automatically craned as she ambled to her Bronco. Carole, holding the nozzle in the aperture of the gas tank, unwittingly glanced up as her husband was pulling the door. She saw what she saw. Farley, eyes released from the magnetic storm, saw her seeing. There goes Christmas, he thought. Carole jerked the nozzle from the hole. Pinkish gas squirted to the ground. There goes Christmas, Farley thought again, seeing in his wife's face the imminent string of mean mornings, necrotic nights and harrowed days that he knew followed such happenings. In the past against Carole's onslaughts, Moses had yodeled long and hard about man, men, me, mind, metaphysics, mystery and myth in an effort to bring peace over the land. But peace, he now knew, was not a thing he could make; it came or it didn't, like a storm over a snowless ski resort in December. He was powerless to coat the slopes with glorious powder. Moses could implore nature but not change it. Part the waters of the seas? Make snow? Joketh not, he thought. I can't even get a clean freeway latrine. Wife will wail while wisdom wishes nothing other. Prior years would have produced gnashing of four layers of teeth, but Farley had learned to shut up. Carole, he reasoned, was like the weather: it gets cold, put on ear muffs; it warms up, take off your clothes. But fretteth not the growling or empty skies.

"Come on kids, back to the space ship," he said as they left the Mini-Market. He had made the mistake of buying one five-piece pack of Bazooka. The children were fighting over opening-rights as they climbed in the back with Freda.

"Stop it! Stop the howling!" Carole shouted, turning her steely eyes past Farley. Her forehead was creased and the soft outline round her lips had pulled to a tight pinch. Farley reached back and intercepted the pack of gum. He gave Rosanne a piece. Then Ricky screamed that the first should be his. It is written, Moses thought, that being second is not for the child. He touched his wife's elbow and offered her a token of peace, a piece of Bazooka wrapped in paper pink and blue. With thorns sticking to the vowels, his wife screeched, "Save it for one of your teenyboppers!" Moses pushed gently on the throttle and the family rejoined the road that wended toward Paradise.

Through the windshield he looked over the land. It was mostly flat and the people mostly dead. They were south of Chico in orchard country. The road was single lane in each direction and it was not quite dark. A hawk on a purring fence, he looked over the land. He saw clearly—in spite of the falling night—that the people were mostly dead. Those that weren't soon would be. Others would replace and be dead in their turn. His children were napping behind him, his wife respecting silence beside him. He with himself looking over the land. When the hawk looks over the land, is it with itself? he wondered. Or is it a mere looking? Not looking out and back in, but just out. The longer Moses lived, the more he looked out. Am I hawk-like? he questioned, looking in, then looking back out over the land, over the dead. But isn't death only in the looking in? The looking in is the building of the I, the great I that is built and nurtured and fed with tautologically inflated thoughts. Then the looking in goes Oh no, *I* am going to die. But looking out builds no I. Looking out looks out until it stops looking, until the light goes out and it retires to nest. Here there is no death.

The Volvo runs into Chico and Moses makes three or four extra turns to drive past the gym at Chico State. He slows the car to 15 mph and eases through the parking lot. Here, he thinks, he played his best games when he was only looking out. Like Chamberlain when he scored a hundred, thinking of nothing, like in a trance. He hadn't slept the night before, he said later. No thought of the *I* doing. Only *doing*. Here there is no defeat. The looking in inflates the I, takes it, brakes it, breaks it. But when a shotgun blast burns through the hawk on the purring fence, this isn't death. It's but a warm finger on the light switch.

Through the windshield, Moses looks into the night. The Volvo climbs the curves as the foothills rise from Chico to Paradise. Everybody from Homer to Heidegger dead and who knows how many went before Homer. What protects the living from the dead? What keeps the I thinking about dinner or the price of lettuce or love or coupling instead of turning to the deep. The I, Moses thinks looking into the night, is its own protection. As it inflates, it takes itself to be bigger than death, deeper than the deep. Then when the shotgun blast approaches, fear grips the I, toys with it like cat with mouse, inward it looks and reels, this fearing I at itself, until the buckshot slides through the heart and death is called death. But I, Moses, bring news that death is not opposite of life. Eyes that look out die not. Deflate the inward I and eternity's warm finger will hold the switch in the ON position. Heaven help the 20th century, the age of psychology, the age of stars, of overrating, the age of the obsessed inflated I. The hawk prays as it looks out on the night from the purring fence. Moses, *oiseau de nuit*. Moses, *Falco peregrinus*.

GRANDPA! GRANDMA! Look! Come and look! I got it! I got the telescope and the Lego pirate ship!" Ricky is pulling his loving Grandpa from his bed. Grandpa sleeps closest to the door, otherwise he would be pulling Grandma. Grandpa rises from the sheets in three stages: he must lift his back and straighten it until he sits on the edge of the bed; he raises his buttocks keeping his knees angled and putting his hands to his waist and pushing his lower spine with his thumbs; the last thrust from his hamstrings and thighs allows him to stand erect and prepare to walk. The morning pain shoots through the arches in his feet. Ricky tugs at his pajama bottoms and Grandpa follows him out of the room.

Ricky was first awake. He had been allowed to sleep on the living room couch next to the kaleidoscopic twinkle of the Christmas tree. Santa's delivery had hence been a tricky affair, albeit successful. Ricky pulled Grandpa to his knees to admire his treasures at close range.

Grandma McOmber and Rosanne, hand in hand, came down the three steps into the sunken living room. Rosanne eyed the lion and elephant grazing beside the tree. She ran to them and in one motion grabbed each around the neck—elephant in left arm, lion in right—pulling their chins to hers. "My woo-woos," she said to nobody.

Carole and Farley were still asleep in the guest room at the back of the house. Farley's prognosis of a wrecked Noël didn't hold up. For two hours she had been silent—from the gas station to Chico. But after Farley drove past his old basketball playing ground, something flicked off the sclerotic temper. They didn't speak until they got to Pentz Drive, but from Chico to Paradise Carole's face resumed its previous luster. Then when they drove into her parent's driveway she said, "I loved your legs. They were the only pair directly descended from the giraffe."

Dinner had been turkey, mashed potatoes, sage dressing, Brussel sprouts, and two bottles of Christian Brothers' finest. Dessert was raspberry pie and cognac and carols round the tree. After Santa came and drank his glass of milk on the chimney, he found Carole in the bed, warm and monostomous, ready to perform their most appreciated gymnastics. The spirit of giving was upon them both. Their gifts exchanged, Farley sunk happily into sleep thinking that if anything is overrated, it's orgasm. Carole stayed awake longer thinking she could have used another.

⌒⌒

Sɪᴛ ᴏɴ ɪᴛ, " he said. "It might help."

"If you really think so," she said.

"Something better," he said.

"How long have you had it?" she asked, taking off her coat after setting the bread on the table.

"Since I got up," he said.

"When was that?"

"Probably half an hour ago."

"Oh."

"Sit on it, okay."

"Joyeux Noël first."

"Joyeux might be Noël if I can get rid of this fucking headache."

She sat on the bed.

It was Christmas as well in the small kitchenless room on the Rue de Seine in Paris. Unseasonably the skies blasted blue, the white of the neighborhood buildings gleaming like drying paint. Christmas Eve had wrapped the city in howling winds and sheets of rain. The storm had blown by, but David Jorgensen had yet to notice. He was lying on his back on the floor on a stained glaucous carpet in the small kitchenless room. On his forehead rested the thick walnut board that was the side of the bed. When she sat on the bed above his head, the board dug a thin ridge across his skull and his pain became one of a different kind. She kept part of her weight on her legs, shifting it to her buttocks when he said *more* and dropping it back toward her feet when he said *that's enough*.

David Jorgensen and Cybil Dawson were in Paris as doctor and patient are at a surgical table. Doctor needs patient; patient needs doctor. David had had to get the hell out of America because Elizabeth had broken his heart and Farley had rattled his brain, a brain that was surely predisposed to rattle. California was no pot in which to stew for a love-slaughtered metaphysically sliced lamb. The cafés, galeries, churches, parks, boulevards and cinemas of the Latin Quarter have served well to provide a temporary theater for many a miscast American. Cybil Dawson had read Beckett, Ionesco, Gide, Genet, and Sartre in her Midwestern high school while the other students were exchanging saliva at the proms. She took her straight A's west and saw in David a potential bedfellow under the vast canopy of the absurd. When Elizabeth gave David nothing more than friendship, Cybil slid into the slit in his heart, copped his virginity, carried him off to Paris, and sat on the bed on his head or absorbed his juices when the need arose. The migraines far outnumbered the erections, but Cybil Dawson didn't mind. She was in Paris breathing the same air as her provisional prophets, speaking French with people who pretended to share her belief in a world without sense, and sleeping in the same kitchenless room with a soft, sensitive, one-eared male.

"That's enough," he said. "I mean I think you can get off now." She stood, then knelt to kiss him and whisper Merry Christmas into his ear.

"Yeah, you too. I got you something. It's here under the bed." He reached and pulled out a plastic bag. "Here."

It was Bernard Malamud's collection of stories called *Rembrant's Hat*. "I read the one, 'The Letter,' standing up in the bookstore the other day. I thought of you."

"Thanks," she said and she gave him another kiss and then a reproduction of Miro's *Femme, oiseaux devant le soleil*.

Christmas day and the sun were kind to David after they left their room to walk along the Seine. They wandered back toward their neighborhood up the Rue Dauphine to the Boulevard St. Germain. They entered a church where an organist was saluting Bach and things holy from David's past. He and Cybil took seats a few rows from the front. He looked at Christ on the cross, but soon he saw Farley sitting atop his desk. I doubt Mr. Farley has migraines, he thought. And he remembered once after class when he and Elizabeth were lingering and Moses threw a hand through his mane and said, "Don't let your thinking nail you to anybody's cross—including your own. Uncertainty might be the only real key to sanity."

When they left the church the sky was California blue. It even smelled like home. David took Cybil to a round wooden table in a café where they sat and got drunk.

B EING, THOUGHT FARLEY as he peered between trees on the thin muddy gravel road somewhere in the hills behind his in-law's house. Then he cupped his hands and shouted, "Freda, FREEE-DAAA." Freda had treated herself to a fox chase for Christmas. After a lunch of baked ham, string beans, and scalloped potatoes, Farley and Freda had gone for a walk. The fox, tail floating like a feather over a sheet of pine needles, had stopped, turned its head downhill toward the man-dog shuffle, and galloped away. Freda had stared into the fox's stare until the fox moved. As she began her chase, Farley thought they should name a car after her.

She had not come back. It was nearing night and Farley's call had been reduced to habit. Sometimes now he inserted a tender invective—a dammit or for-krise-sakes-its-krismas—between *Freda* and *FREEEE-DAAAA*. In any case, the interval between his cries had lengthened and he began to think of other things. Being, at present, had come to mind. That there is something and not nothing. But this, Farley mused, can only be thought about for so long, so often. *Freda...FREEE-DAAAAA*. Then it came back, the thought that there is anything at all, and raised hair on his spine. The pines shook inside the early evening breeze. The breeze shook inside the pines. She may be dead, he thought, not really believing—Freda a loser in the third round to the ferocious fox, blood scorching her black-on-white-on-beige fur, her tongue hanging limp into the ground. But he didn't really believe it. He saw her—the fox long gone—sniffing the forest for food. She'd be hungry after the chase and dining hour was near. She was licking water from rain puddles. She would point her ears on hearing what might have been a pine cone fall. Then he saw her see a squirrel and bark beneath the tree where the squirrel had climbed until she couldn't see the squirrel anymore. He saw her tongue slide from her jaw as she wandered from the tree, tired, her ears leaning sideways. She stopped and looked sideways, no longer knowing where to walk. Farley did the same and saw himself doing it, though he saw neither Freda nor himself. He stopped on the muddy gravel road and looked sideways no longer knowing where to walk. *Freda...FREEE-DAAA.* The breeze and the pine trees blew inside each other and Farley remembered that he didn't like walking in the dark where there weren't street lights. It was time to give up. Pentz Drive was down, so he headed down it before it was fully dark.

Freda was looking for Farley but she didn't mind the dark. The chase had taken her over a hill. When she came back Farley was gone. She drank from a rain puddle, then stood with her head bowed and her ears horizontal to the ground. She had found no food. She had walked a large circle before coming back up and over the hill. She was lost in that Farley was not there, but the forest was full of the breeze that brought her scents of rabbit and fox and deer and woodchuck. When light came back to the forest, Freda found a small farm where she slept behind the barn until she heard a door and a person. She approached the person with her nose down and her tail bouncing low to the ground. The person fed her, gave her water, called the police, and pet her with hands smaller than Farley's.

As he walked down Pentz Drive, Farley thought it was a good thing he hadn't found Freda. Had he, after three hours of looking, he was certain his wife wouldn't have believed his story. She would have dreamt him elsewhere, in circumstances doing what violated her bedraggled sense of self. Take me home, country road, he thought as he strolled on the left side of the blacktop. A dog is always home where there are two bowls daily filled and a hand under the chin, he mused.

Nearing his in-laws' house he remembered his dream of the night before. He had put a live turkey in an oven to cook. He had turned the temperature to 350 degrees. Two hours later he opened the oven with the intention of basting. The turkey was exactly how it had been when he put it in. Its eyes stared straight out of its unmoving head. Farley woke up before he re-closed the oven.

He felt the weight of those eyes as he pulled the gate in front of the path to the McOmber house. When he saw his wife, her eyes were bathetic balls, more pathetic than bathos. He saw nothing behind them. There is nothing behind sentimentality, he thought, nothing but human life. He wondered what he meant and he was tired. The children lamented their lost dog until Grandma gave them ice cream.

His wife's anger angered him. It was a habit that he felt he had nothing to do with.

"Don't you care about the dog?" he asked.

"I never have," she said.

꒜

"Y ES, DAVID."

"Mr. Farley, you said last lesson that this lesson you'd tell us what you thought man's greatest errors were if we reminded you."

"That's right, I did," Farley says taking off his charcoal herringbone coat and sitting on his desk. "Is anybody still interested?" He isn't sure he is anymore, but he'll see if they are.

"Man's Greatest Intellectual Errors: An Appendix to Metaphysics 101, Room 424, B Building, Professor L.C. Farley PH.D.E.F.G.H.I.J." (Elizabeth laughs into her hair.)

"Man's first intellectual error—and here when I say intellectual I mean instinctual because back then nobody was dumb enough to think there was a difference (David Jorgensen laughs)—was standing up." (Farley slowly gets down on all fours. Most of the class laugh. Everybody juggles his or her buttocks to get a better view.) "Here, in this position, there were very few backaches. The only backaches were a result of branches or large coconuts or rocks falling on the backs of our forefathers. Since 56,000 B.C—the day man first invented two legs—the human race has been plagued with back problems, particularly lower back and last vertabrae." (Farley rolls over on his back and kicks his four limbs toward the ceiling.) "It so happens that when a human being has an acute pain in his back, he is unable to get his soul to venture into higher realms of being such as bowling, nuclear physics, or chasing women in bars. The bad back inflicts a very high percentage of humanity and has done much to brake, that is B-R-A-K-E, the cultural and intellectual progress of mankind. The only art people with bad backs can produce are poems about pain or X-rays that can only be appreciated by orthopedists and radiologists. (Christine Lasenger thinks Mr. Farley is crazy and wonders if it's too late to drop the class. Max Lippett thinks this is the most fun he's had at the university since the Mud Bowl football game.) "In fact, (Farley is back on all fours and crawling) if I might be so bold, I'd say that man was so stupid that not only did he stand up, but he started to build pyramids and cathedrals and railroads, forcing himself to carry things like large pieces of rock and granite and steel ties. And kings started asking to be carried and weight-lifting and volleyball were invented and so forth. I'm sure you can see the implications and consequences and dysteleological ramifications."

(Farley stands up again. David looks at Elizabeth who looks at Farley's dirty trousers. David writes "disteleogical" on a notebook.)

"And the second greatest intellectual error—I speak chronologically—was a Greek one. Plato—not the one in the James Dean film—decided that man was not part of nature and he told all his friends that on life's totem pole they were all above rocks and olive trees and scorpions. Plato's friends all looked at each other and said, 'Hey far out...groovy...if I can't be an Olympian God at least I don't have to be part of nature.' (Max Lippett is laughing in Christine Lasenger's lap.) Well, to make a long story short, Plato's friends all went off and told all their friends and before Zeus could say 'zap' people everywhere from Zurich to Zanzibar to Luckenback, Texas believed they were not part of nature. Now you might ask why is it such a big deal not to be part of nature. But if you think about it for a while you might see why. Anybody care to think about it for awhile?"

(The students don't move and are no longer laughing.)

"Okay, then listen for a little longer and then I'm sure the bell will rescue you." (Farley is enjoying himself. But his tone now becomes more serious.)

"If man believes he is not part of nature, this radically influences the way he lives and dies. First, let's see how it affects how man sees other men. When we look at *nature*—plants, animals, oceans, clouds, etc.—we do not expect it to be anything other than what it is. Its being and behavior is accepted because we think it behaves *naturally*—it could not do or be otherwise. We might want a cloud to come or go away, but we do not really believe that the cloud could be doing other than what it is doing. Once we put man outside of *nature* we expect him to act in certain ways, depending on our system of beliefs in the good, the right, the wrong and so forth. We see man's actions as continually good or bad depending on whether or not they correspond to our notions of morality. Morality makes no sense in *nature* because we say that *nature* cannot be other than what it is. But man, seeing himself outside of this realm, wages a constant war with his fellowmen because he perceives their behavior to be other than what it ought to be. In Christianity, man is rewarded or punished because it's *his* fault. Our judicial system is similar in so far as it would make no sense to *judge* a man whom we thought could do nothing other than what he does. The same is not true for Biblical cows. We cage animals or we shoot them or we spray them or we ignore them, but we never judge them. If man saw and perceived his fellows to be part of nature, his whole mode of social interaction would be different. Society as it is today would certainly not be." (A hand goes up. David's.)

"Yes."

"How do you see us, Mr. Farley, or your wife and kids?"

"I was wondering if you'd ask. Actually it depends on my mood or what day it is. Or maybe it depends on who you are. I'd say that in general I see mankind like I see the cloud or the Biblical cow. Man is there and can be nothing other. In fact I don't really think that man thinking he is not part of nature is *wrong* in the sense that he *should* think otherwise. I think this is just the way he developed like some cows developed black and white spots. For me, I guess the only exception is in what I'd call love. For some reason, though it may be nonsense, I expect the person I've chosen to live with to do certain things. This might be because the person you love is your chosen mirror in some sense, and when that mirror doesn't show you certain things, you get pissed off, to use an expression everybody understands. My wife is really the only person I hold responsible. I know it's not logical, but neither was the score of last week's 49er game. Actually every now and then my fellow men do get to me, but it's probably just after a hard day's work." ("You work?" Max Lippett thinks.) "As for my kids—and you—I definitely see you as the most beautiful clouds ever to grace the heavens."

"So you think New York City is part of nature?" Max Lippett asks.

"As much as a beehive," Farley says.

"Mr. Farley," David adds, "at the beginning of the lesson you said something about instinct and intellect being the same thing. Is that what you believe?"

"Believe is a big word, but if man is set in nature like a cactus in the desert, then I'd be inclined to put the mind in there with the milk."

(The class is quiet. Farley hears himself exhale.)

"Now let's try to imagine how such a view might influence man's sense of himself. If I am part of nature, and this then means that my being is no freer than the cloud or the Biblical cow, how will I treat myself? It strikes me that the first thing to go is guilt. Guilt is feeling that you shouldn't have done something—or that you should have and didn't—because either you consider your action or the consequences of your action to be bad. If I think that my being is part of a great cosmic necessity, then I am not going to feel guilty about what I do. I might look at what I've done and say, 'Oh boy, I'm in a fix,' or 'Okay, let's try to fix this mess we're in,' but I won't feel guilt over what I've done. I might wish I had been a creature that had acted otherwise, but that has nothing to do with guilt. Guilt is only possible when I *know* or believe that I could have done otherwise. Nature can be nothing other than what it is, so if I'm part of nature I could not have done otherwise and guilt would cease to be a notion in my life."

(Elizabeth raises her hand.)

"Maybe I shouldn't ask, but do you ever feel guilty, Mr. Farley?"

"It may sound strange, but not really. Not for a long time anyway. That's not to say I don't think about what I do before doing it—I'd say I always try to do what I think Mr. Farley ought to do—but I *know* that my thinking about what I do might very well be something that I don't control. You remember when we discussed thinking and what it is. Well, here, the mystery of thinking is part of how I perceive *Me* and *My doing*."

(Max Lippett thinks that he's never going to feel guilty again about laying chicks or getting drunk. What he doesn't know is that now he might lay chicks differently and get drunk differently.)

"Now I know," Farley goes on, "that it's very difficult to conceive of the world in this way. It goes against all that you've been taught all your lives probably. But when you walk out of this class—just for a minute—try to imagine all the people you see and their actions and constructions in the same way you would see beavers or birds or waves on a shore. Just try. See if the world feels different. See if you feel different in it."

(Farley looks at his watch and sees there are five more minutes left in the period. He doesn't want to talk anymore so he says to an approving class...)

"Man's third greatest intellectual error was making these damn periods five minutes too long. Have a good weekend. See you on Monday."

Farley Lay in the bathtub looking at the design on the tile wall in front of him. He had been living on Peter Street for four months and for the first time he noticed that the design looked like Donald Duck. The tile maker had intended something resembling flowers, Farley thought, but the result was that every fourth square now brought to mind the words, "suffering succotash." His bath time would never be the same.

In the two months since Christmas, Farley had done little else than what he saw himself now doing: amusing himself with what went through his head and body. Heidegger hadn't received a finger of attention and his concern for why water turns white when it falls had fared no better. "Suffering succotash," he thought as he looked at the wall. Then he wondered if "suffering succotash" had been Daffy's words and not Donald's.

He had spent the first week in January painting in his kitchen. There was enough room for the easel. He did ten canvases of acrylic blotches and lines mixed with pastel crayon scribblings. He noticed he had used a lot of red, green, and black, and that he was leaving more of the canvas naked than he used to. Such unpainted space was often attributed to something about breathing, but Farley thought the only part of a painting that needed air was the painter himself. For once he liked what he had done so he had hung the pictures, one at a time, on a steel nail in the living room wall. He had left each up for a week, Saturday to Saturday. This gave him a reason to look at the calendar and keep track of when it was his time to be with the kids. Carole had taken in a graduate assistant in agronomy from Africa that she had met at a Christmas party given by one of Farley's esteemed colleagues. Farley had not attended. He had stayed home on Peter Street with the children to look at toy catalogues and eat popcorn. Now that the agronomist was occupying his old half of the bed on a regular basis, he stayed away from Moraga. Carole brought him the kids on Saturday morning, at which time he put a different painting on the wall.

("He gives me everything you didn't," she said one February Saturday through the window of the Volvo.

"Everything?" Farley countered. "Now what might that be?"

"He listens to me. He thinks I have something to say."

"I never said you didn't have anything to say. I just didn't agree with what you said."

"Well, he listens."

"I listened too."

"The only thing you ever listened to was yourself talking."

"I listen. I just don't like what I hear."

"What do you like, Farley?"

"What I don't hear."

"You're hopeless.")

After ten weeks he left the last picture on the wall. He had entitled it *Life Still* though it looked nothing like fruit on a table. The top of the canvas had a green splotch that he had surrounded with splashes of black, white, and blue. On the lower right was another green form about the size and shape of a bowling pin. Here he added halos of black and red. He finished the painting by brushing a thick yellow line horizontally in the middle of the canvas. His eyes presently went from the duck on the tile through the open bathroom door to the picture in his living room.

("Maybe realizing you're hopeless is a necessary condition for living," Farley said through the closing Volvo window.

"I'm happy, Farley. I haven't felt this way for years."

"Is a man a necessary condition for your happiness?"

"It helps. I haven't seen you keeping your fingers out of the pie."

"I'm not sure anymore. Sometimes I think this business of the two sexes is just a big cosmological nuisance. If mating weren't part of living, we'd have a lot more time for other things."

"Like what?"

"Being alone."

Carole closed the window.)

"Suffering succotash," Farley said to the ducks. A cosmological nuisance, he thought. What if our way of mating was a huge mistake? What if the last two thousand years of history had been a coupling aberration. Maybe man and woman were absolutely not made to go through life they way they now do. Courtship, love, fidelity, infidelity, marriage, divorce, watching, peeping, pining, paining, pairing, re-pairing, worry, wonder, want, sin, sex, single, married, martyred, mistressed, masturbate, penetrate, penis, pill, suck, fuck, chuck, hump, pump, dump, yes, no, baby say it ain't so.

Farley lay in the last of the bath suds and had a vision of a world that operated differently. But then he wondered if anyone was living there. Wolves or coyotes. Maybe. Lizards. Fish. Dogs. Porcupines. Pigs. He didn't know. House sparrows. Flamingos. Locusts. Mallards. Leaf-hoppers. Black grouse. Mountain goat. The ancient Egyptians. The Greeks. He doubted. Maybe they didn't get started making out in drive-ins or meticulously parting their hair for a third-grader, but they likely lived the same man/woman hodgepodge. What hodgepodge? he thought looking into the sudless murkiness in which his dormant tube lay like a buoy. What do I know, other than that the whole thing might be a mistake? Nature gone haywire and California sporting seventy percent divorce rates. Something just tells me that there's a hitch in there somewhere. Maybe there's no such thing as two sexes. Maybe for every living being there is a different sex. Farley had thought about thinking far more than he had thought about man, woman, and the coupling of angelfish and antelope.

His pecker had been happily at rest for weeks, but for a few early morning lunges into the sheets. He tried to rouse it before he pulled the plug. Nothing doing. He pulled the plug then looked at one of the ducks. The pained succotash must have belonged to Daffy, he thought.

DAVID JORGENSEN looked like Robert Redford except for the one ear and a less squared chin. The comparison had flattered him, especially in conjunction with the film *Jeremiah Johnson* in which Redford had sported a loner's beard and hair the length of drinking straws. As soon as he and Cybil walked out of the theater, he commanded his facial and head hair to grow. The beard came out in patches and jerks at first, but by his third year at the university it had begun to hold its own to Redford's. His hair grew in flowing waves that looked like stalks of grain that were forever in the grips of autumn. He kept himself this way until he and Cybil decided to leave for Paris. By then he no longer wanted to look like Redford, so he got a crew cut and shaved his face. Since Redford had never made a film with a Marine coiffure, David drew fewer comparative remarks. He tried to feel that he was more himself, but actually he was only less Redford.

In Paris, David was seen as a distant cousin to Vincent Van Gogh. This dismayed him when he had picked up enough French to realize that the locals on the Rue de Seine were calling him "notre petit Vincent" as he'd walk from the boulangerie to the kiosque for the *Herald Tribune* and past the art galleries back to his room. His melancholic demeanor had as much to do with the comparison as the tangle of skin that had once been his left ear. Cybil preferred her beloved with the Van Gogh stamp. Pessimism was her game and who in the world cast a heavier shadow than the dead artist? When she sat on the bed that was planted in David's forehead, she saw herself in the throes of intellectual orgasm.

As Farley stepped out of the bathtub after his run around the reservoir, David was ordering Cybil off the bed.

"It's bullshit," he said. "I'm sick of it."

"Me?" Cybil said.

"Not you, but you're part of it."

"Part of what?"

"What I'm sick of. What the hell good is a brain for if it takes what it sees and turns it to shit. You know what I think? I think that some people are bright enough to see that life isn't what Sunday School made it out to be, but they're not bright enough to go past that realization to climb out of the slime. I want out. You're never going to sit on this bed again with me under it. I remember my father quit smoking from one day to the next. Well, I'm quitting the life of the pseudo-brain that walks outside in the rain because rain is supposed to be *bad* weather and I'm the type that likes to get wet because it makes him sick. Fuck it. I'm sick of it. Maybe Gene Kelly was right—if you're going to walk in the rain, you might as well sing in it. I've been wallowing in the mud for three years now—since I thought I was so smart that I realized that maybe the alphabet I learned in kindergarten wasn't the key to eternal truth and that maybe mother love was an instinct rather than a gift of God."

"I thought mother love was a mimicry of *The Donna Reed Show*," Cybil said laughing while tears welled in her eyes.

"Maybe. But whatever it is, it's likely not what we learned in Sunday School. Don't you see what I mean?"

"See, no. Feel, yes. David, you're the only thing I've loved since my gold fish died," she said, falling into a heated sob on the bed.

David rubbed the crease across his brow. It's not worth it, he thought, thinking that if life is a one-shot affair, then I better start throwing my pennies at a different plate. If I don't know, then I don't need to not know in pain. Why not live in the fog with a smile on your face? At least step away from the guillotine and join the carnival. Maybe not join, but at least be amused. Bless Mr. Farley who, if I read him right, taught neither the up nor down, the high nor low, the lucid nor the crazed, nor the ought, nor the might have been. He looked at Cybil, a human heap.

"Kiss me," she mumbled. He thought her marriage with the absurd broke up when her love cracked. Love as a necessary condition for solid pessimism.

"No," he said.

"Kiss me, David," she repeated rolling on her back and lifting her hands.

"Why?"

"Because you must."

He kissed her, but the next morning it was she who had left. She had packed while he slept and slipped out while the streets of Paris were empty of all but the garbage collecters and a few slivers of light.

FREDA HAD BEEN returned to Farley after much ado. The woman on the farm outside of Paradise had called the police who had told her to see if there was a phone number or an address on the dog's person. There was—the Farley home in Moraga. The woman immediately called Moraga, though she wondered how a dog in Paradise could have a 415 area code. It happened that Adoula, the African agronomist, was in the house setting roses on the kitchen table for his lover's return. He hesitantly answered the phone and told the woman that he was a guest in the house, but as far as he knew there was no dog named Freda in the house. When he said "in the house" the woman said, "No, not in the house you're in, because Freda is here with me in my house." The agronomist was confused but wanted to do nothing wrong. His English was far from perfect but he said clearly, "If the Freda animal is in your house, why you want to know if the animal in my house?" The woman explained in rapid syllables (having never spoken to a real foreigner before she had no idea that somebody in America did not speak the same tongue as she) that she knew the dog wasn't in his house, but wondered if it lived there.

"Nobody live here now," Adoula said.

"What do you mean nobody lives in your house?" the woman barked.

"I mean I not live here but woman that live here not here because it Christmas in America," Adoula said nervously.

"Who is the woman?" the woman said.

"She very butiful and have hair like many rings since she go to the beauty pallor with me last week."

The woman hung up the phone thinking maybe the nut on the other end could trace her number and hack her to shedded wheat on a rainy night. Adoula had only wanted to be kind and respectful.

The woman kept Freda for two weeks and enjoyed her until Freda broke into her chicken coop and tore up two of her chickens. She wanted to kill the dog, but wondered—in a moment of moral quandary—if maybe she hadn't dialed the wrong number two weeks before. So before she put her Winchester to Freda's head, she called the 415 number again. Carole answered. Freda was spared. Farley came to get her the next day.

Farley had missed the dog, had missed her chewing sticks that she brought back from the reservoir and her spitting bark on the carpet in the living room. He had missed the dog food section in Safeway. He had missed her begging next to him while he ate cheese and drank wine in the evening. He missed tossing the ends and corners of hunks of Monterey Jack and Gruyère to the floor. He missed Freda's ears rising to attention as she awaited another piece. He missed the curve of her haunches.

"Let's go," he said to her, having dressed after his bath. "Let's go break bread at one of our country's finer hamburger drive-in establishments. I'm hungry." Freda shook her buttocks and jumped at his legs. The phone rang.

"Farley, your mother called," Carole said with business-like direction.

"And..."

"She wants you to call her. Didn't you tell her you'd moved out?"

"No."

"Why not?"

"I didn't want her to worry."

"Well, she seems worried about herself. She wasn't real clear on the phone. In fact, she asked me twice if we'd had a good time at Christmas."

"I called her on Christmas."

"I know. That's why I'm telling you. She acted a little confused. I think you better call her."

"Did you tell her I was out?"

"No. I told her you were playing golf."

"I was running."

"How the hell should I know?" Carole had Adoula in the TV room. She was losing a thread of the patience that she had left in her banished husband. The spool was near the end. "Listen, I've gotta go. But I suggest you call your mother."

Farley hung up the phone and wondered how much of his life he'd spent listening to his wife's voice. Just now it had sounded like the voice of somebody's secretary, a voice he'd heard before and knew, but couldn't put a face to. Time may heal, he thought, but it can also widen the gorge.

W<small>HEN</small> CAROLE MET Adoula at the Christmas party, she had been discussing C.G. Jung in a standing position. The living room had been deprived of most of its chairs to make room for the guests. The Sonia Delauney rug had been removed as well as a large glass fish. Carole was talking to Arthur Fryer about Jung's concept of anima when she said, "I've always noticed it in Farley." Adoula, who was standing behind her, turned and said, "I work me too with barley." Carole broke into a half-drunk high-pitched laughter which had Adoula thinking she was making fun of his English.

"Did I say wrong?" he asked, dropping his tender eyes to the shiny wood floor.

"You say right," Carole said, still laughing and pivoting a half turn away from Arthur Fryer. "You couldn't have say righter." Adoula still didn't know if she was making fun of him, but he was glad he had met someone other than the head of the Agronomy Department.

"I sorry if I speak wrong," he said, "but I just come from my country last week. Do you know of barley?"

"I was talking about Farley," Carole said, putting her free hand on Adoula's shoulder. "He once was what we call a husband. Mine in fact." With her other hand she drank chilled Chablis.

Adoula understood the language reasonably well. As with most foreigners, his comprehension was far superior to his expression. "You have no more husband?" he asked.

"Maybe I never did."

"I have not wife."

"I have not husband." She was past half-drunk.

"Have you study barley?"

"As much as you study Farley?"

"Farley not your husband?"

"Farley not my husband. You want be my husband?" Carole finished her glass, then, though tipsy, fell back into normal speech. "Sorry, it's just been one of those last few months. Make that years. I really wasn't making fun of you." She grabbed his arm and took him toward the smoked salmon table.

They found two chairs in the kitchen. Carole sat Adoula down and tried to learn what she could about barley and coming to America via Africa. She didn't know where Gabon was and he had never heard of Paradise. Neither seemed to care what the other was saying. Both seemed happy to speak and be heard.

When the party ended, Carole was sober enough to drive home and offered to give Adoula a lift. When he politely refused saying the Agronomy Chairman had promised him a way home, Carole felt a stirring just above her navel. Three days later she bought him a sweater. A week later they had lunch together which they punctuated with cross-cultural kisses and "see you soons."

The children had quickly become accustomed to having Adoula in the house. He mowed the lawn, tied the newspapers, swept the driveway, trimmed the high hedges, raked leaves, and hosed down the Volvo with the kids reveling within. The neighbors thought he was a new gardner. Ricky and Rosanne thought he talked funny.

Their romance would wither with the arrival of spring, but they made the most of January and February. They spent their time together laughing and love-making. Carole needed a flood of both to take her mind off Farley. Adoula would chuckle, pour wine, and say, "Let's dwit baby." Once the Department Chairman asked him how he was coming with his research and he answered, "Research smooth like cherry wine." The kids being in school gave them mornings free. Adoula usually went to the library in the afternoon, but he was back by dinner time.

Carole joined Adoula in the TV room after talking to Farley. He was focused on a "Leave It To Beaver" rerun. Eddie Haskell had broken a window with a baseball and had stacked the blame on the Beaver. Wally didn't know where to throw his loyalty, but everyone knew where it would land. TV drama was in full bloom. Carole curled an arm around Adoula's shoulder as Eddie shoved Beaver toward the rose bushes. Adoula mechanically set his hand between Carole's legs. Eddie and Beaver had momentarily pushed his lover's thighs into a far corner of his brain.

"I like this Eddie Rascal," he said trying to draw her into his cocoon.

"Your English is leaping and bounding. Pretty soon you can write your own shows." When they first met she'd suggested TV as the quickest way to a command of the language and now she was beginning to regret her suggestion. As they began to spend less time working up orgasms, Adoula had filled the space with the slobbery Sony. At first Carole had been amused, but of late she had considered finding a way to break the machine.

"Eddie wants always to get trouble for the Beaver."

"And the Beaver wants always to be a good boy, right? Adoula, haven't you seen enough TV today?"

"This is only my second one."

"Second what?"

"Second show tonight. No problem, honey."

Before Ward Cleaver came home from work, Eddie owned up to the window. Wally had kept evil at bay. Beaver was spared the pain of the lie. Love filled the Cleaver dining-room.

Do YOU LOVE, Farley? Anything or anybody?"

Farley poured wine into the empty glasses on the coffee table. Elizabeth took hers and snuggled, feet up, into a corner of the couch.

"If you weren't my favorite ex-student, I'd lie to you. But you are. So I won't." Farley lowered himself to the rug and lay under Elizabeth's feet.

"So...?"

"Why don't you waddle your tongue first. I'm interested."

"Sorry, I asked you first. You're the teacher, remember?"

"Nothing worth knowing can be taught. Remember?"

"Who's talking about knowing. Just teach like a good boy." Elizabeth had come to trust Farley and felt she could let things roll.

"Too bad I've got such a small audience. Maybe I should record myself and play it back to a full class." He reached back and rubbed a few toes much smaller than his.

"I'll try to make myself plural," she said.

"Do you remember that day David reminded me to talk about what I considered the great intellectual errors of Western man? Well, I intentionally left out the one about romantic love. I thought it should be left to experience."

"Maybe I should wish you'd talked about it. Instead of wanting you, maybe I'd have wanted out."

"Maybe, but I can't see why. Let's start with a thesis and work toward particulars. I'd say romantic love is really just masturbation *à deux*. You can do it alone or you can do it by twos. Alone they tell you your hand's going to fall off. By twos you're supposed to be floating with the angels. You're Adam and Eve without the apple.

When I look back at my own life—from my first girlfriend at age four to you—I'm beginning to wonder if there's not some fixed apparatus in me that goes off every now and then and ends up by pulling a woman into my arms. We like to think that desire is an act of freedom, especially when it leads to something fun. The basketball player thinks he's free when he's playing basketball. The preacher thinks he's free when he preaching. The bird watcher feels free when he spying on birds. Same for the lover. He likes to think that that rumbling in his loins is an act of free choice. I doubt it. I'd say it's more like a magnetic storm. When two people get it at the same time we call it love—for a while anyway." Farley grabbed for more toes, but Elizabeth pulled back her foot. "I didn't think you'd take it personally. We're in school remember? You're more than one."

"How am I supposed to take it?"

"Like a woman. Like you did."

"Sometimes I think you destroy everything, Farley."

"Now what might everything be?" He felt for the first time with her a recurrence of Carole. But he knew better than to compare.

"I don't know. Maybe I don't want to know. You demystify everything, that's all."

"Do I? You sure? Go back to the night we ate at El Charro. You didn't seem to feel demystified. You said, 'The horses are galloping!' if I remember correctly. And gallop they did. Maybe you need me and I need you. Just like plants need water. What the hell could be more beautiful than that?" Farley thought she was going to start to cry and she did. He plucked a toe and it stayed in his hand.

"You said..." she sniffled.

"I said you were my favorite ex-student."

"Take me home," she said. "No, don't," she sputtered into the sofa.

PART II

To live alone one must be an animal or God, says Aristotle.
There is yet a third case: one must be both—a philosopher.

Friedrich Nietzsche, *Twilight of the Idols*

MOTHER? FARLEY WONDERS, looking at his across the room in her condominium off the second hole of the Bloomington Country Club in St. George, Utah. Does the earth offer anything holier than a mother? But is the holy a mere function of habit? What human habit is deeper, tighter, more hallowed than one's mother? To be snuggled, held, healed, clothed, fed, called, caressed and wanted near. To have been mothered by a mother until school started, then to be mothered through school until you go away to the university. The kitchen smells, the skin and hair and soap smells. The hand on the hot forehead. The lips on the cheek until you're too big for them. What habit, Farley wonders, is heavier—holier—than the mother? As he looks at her he thinks, If holiness is habit, this does nothing to make it unholy.

She is seventy-five, but for him she never left her thirties. She is withered and hunched as she prepares a sandwich behind the window that opens onto the second fairway. Her maroon slacks look like drapes, drapes that shelter drying bones. She is wearing a sweater though it is warm inside and out. The sweater is the same silver and blue one that Farley gave her when her hair changed and she did nothing to change it back. Her feet fit loosely in her shoes which are 8 and 1/2s because she has not bought any for years. Hallowed be thy name, Farley thinks when she turns and walks toward him with the sandwich on the plate.

"Did you bring your golf clubs?" she asks him for the third time since he arrived the night before.

"Sure did," he says, now knowing that she cannot retain any new information.

"Where are Carole and the children?" she asks again.

"They're in Moraga," he repeats.

"When are they coming?"

"They're not. The kids are in school."

"Don't you have school?"

"I'm on sabbatical."

"Why so?"

"I just needed a break, Mom. Thanks for the sandwich."

Farley wonders if she can live alone much longer. If she can't remember if he's brought his golf clubs, she can't remember if she's put something on the stove or turned on the bath water. He could live with her for awhile. Why not? he thinks.

"How was your flight?" she asks.

"I drove, Mom. It went fine."

"I know there's something wrong with me, Larry. I know I'm not remembering very well. I have seen the doctor and he has talked to you, hasn't he?" Only his mother calls him Larry anymore. He always liked Larry, but it was lost during his last two years in high school when the speaker at games started shouting FAR-LEEEE every time he threaded his fadaway jumpshot or slithered through traffic to bank one off the glass.

"I haven't talked to him, but I will. These things happen. We'll just do what we can."

"When did you say the children are coming?"

"They won't be coming until summer, Mom. They've got school."

"Oh yes, they have."

Farley looks out of the living room window at the red mountain to the north. It looks baked like the clay bowl he made for his parents in crafts class in seventh grade. The mountain bakes in the baby blue oven that is cut rectangular by the bay window. A fleecy cirrus, sliced horizontally like accordion keys, moves right to left through the upper part of the rectangle. It passes, then comes an airplane. The 20th century, Farley thinks as he watches the silver snail crawl. The epoch will one day look like the Middle Ages. Give man a couple hundred more years to maneuver and he'll look back at us—the 20th century dead—and label our planes and pains and cars and notions archaic.

The plane passes. The baby blue smoothed. Mrs. Farley suggests that her son play golf after lunch. Farley loves little more than he loves golf in the heat and red rock of the southern Utah desert. When his parents moved there to retire, he was delighted. The first summer he took Carole, pleasantly pregnant with Ricky, to Bryce Canyon. They stayed at Ruby's Inn and rode horses through the woods to the west rim. He rode behind his wife and watched her waist, still thin, slide from side to side atop the charred squeaky saddle. She had a black and red checkered shirt tucked into her French jeans. He watched the horse's tail and her ponytail flicker until they reached the rim of the canyon. Then he watched lizards scuttle and small birds loop between the shale totems, and he heard the hole in the earth below him whisper infinity into the horses' ears. The horses lumbered like camels.

Carole's mount has followed the airplane through and out of the rectangle.

"I'd love to play," he says.

"Did you bring your clubs?"

"Yeah, Mom." She is back at the sink puttering in her holy sphere, her maroon slacks—much the color of Carole's Volvo— sheltering her drying bones.

FARLEY IS SITTING behind the pulpit wearing black. Shoes borrowed from a friend, turtleneck, silk pants, socks, belt, Oakland Raiders cap with the silver lettering blackened by a felt-pen: all are as black as he could find on short notice. He had decided to lecture on death while reading the *Chronicle* that morning. It is now five to eleven and he has come to class before his students. He unfolds a pair of dark glasses and slides them on. In front of him is a large cardboard box, open at one end, that he found on the way to school at a refrigerator store. He has drawn a cross with the felt-pen on the side that faces the students' desks. At two minutes to eleven he crawls into the box and waits.

The bell. The students trickle in. Farley's head is at the closed end of the box so they are not entirely certain it is within. They take their seats and mumble, joke, and stare at the box waiting for something to happen. The second bell rings. For what is a long four minutes, their teacher lies motionless. Christine Lasenger is scared though she doesn't know why and doesn't want to think about why. Arthur Windell has just come from *Weather and Climate* class and thinks anything is better than stratocumulus clouds and barometric pressure. Elizabeth is not surprised and is anxious to see Farley's face and hear the steady pump of his voice. Max Lippet says softly to no one in particular, "This muthafucker is one blown-out buckaroo." David Jorgensen remembers his grandfather's open coffin with his grandfather lying like a wax fruit and the smell of flowers like he had never smelled before. His underarms are warm and he puts his fingers over the stub that was once his ear.

As Professor Farley worms his way out of the box, his students are silent. He rises like a speaker at a funeral, then speaks: "We are gathered here this morning to honor, remember and commemorate the lives of twenty-eight wonderful young human beings—that is, if nobody's dropped out since last week—and one teacher. I stand before you as a friend of you, the living, and of you, the dead, and as a friend to myself, also both alive and deceased. Moments like these are moments when we reflect...together...on our purpose, the meaning of things, and, more particularly, on the life of those who are no longer with us in the flesh." (Farley gestures to the cardboard box, then takes a deep breath.)

"Friends, what is a man's life...a woman's life...but his works? But what are his works? Are his thoughts his works? Are the Twinkies and chili-dogs he ate and excreted his works? Are his children, in fact, his works? Are works only things which are eventually known by others? Are the deep corners—and the shallow ones—of his soul his works? Can a man even remember his own works? I can't remember 99% of what I've done in life. If we can't remember our own works, how are we supposed to commemorate somebody else's works? But are these important questions, my friends...in the face of the death of him who has worked works? What is important in death? Is death really the opposite of life? Think about it. Are there really opposites in nature? Surely warm is not the opposite of cold, but only a degree of difference in something called temperature. Fast is not the opposite of slow, but only ways to describe variants in something we call motion. Big and little can surely not be opposites in infinite space. So friends...is death really the opposite of life? Are there opposites in nature? Can we presume what death is from what we see life to be?" (Farley points to the refrigerator box and takes off the

Raiders cap and holds it to his chest.) "If we think deeply... deeply, friends...might death be something other than what we normally think it to be. And is death an *It*? If there are no opposites in nature, in being, then let us think of death and life in the same fruit bowl. Life is a banana. Death is a green apple. Now let us meditate and pray silently for a few minutes..."

Farley bows his head. A number of students do the same.

Max Lippet thinks death sucks, but doesn't push it past his lust for Elizabeth.

David Jorgensen wonders about no opposites in nature and thinks Mr. Farley can't be wrong.

Elizabeth likes the dark glasses and asks herself why her teacher isn't an actor in Hollywood or New York. She has taken a class the semester before on the American Indian and thinks there's a relation to what Farley is saying and some of the Navajo theories.

Christine Lasenger still feels fear—fear of something about Farley and his words. How can a man like this be nice? But he is.

Farley puts back on the Raiders cap, looks at the class waiting for questions. There are none, so he goes on.

"How do we think or envision what we call death? Strangely, to say the least. Maybe I should say inconsistently. What do I mean by inconsistently? We are constantly and absolutely surrounded by creatures and existents that *die*—to use the common word. The billions and billions of insects and small animals around us live for minutes or days or weeks, but their lives are ephemeral. Even penguins who go thirty years or people who go seventy are ephemeral, short-lived. And then there are trees, plants, grass, weeds. They come and go and what do we think of them? How do we experience their being and non-being? We feel nothing. Or very little. Every now and then we crusade for minks or polar bears or bald eagles, but in general we feel absolutely nothing with regard to the transformation and destruction around us. We might care about the extinction of a species of lizards, but what about the millions of those lizards that are already long dead and gone. It is not *death* we care about, it is something else. What? Human emotions and concerns are not equipped to deal with the totality of death. What we do is pick out a few instances of disappearance and show concern—for a grandmother or a cat or a porcupine on the highway or a president. This concern is really a concern for what? Might it not only be a concern for what touches us most closely—that is, the thought of our own death? Or our life in the absence of the newly deceased? But this brings us back to how we conceive of our own death—as the opposite of life. And if there are no opposites in nature, have we really any idea of what we are talking about when we speak of life and death? Are we not just concerned with our own little mud pies, our own little perspectives, our own little gardens? Is there anything wrong with this? Can it be otherwise? Is man made to experience death other than this?"

Farley takes off the dark glasses and smiles at the penguins. He puts the glasses back on and says, "Think about it. Enjoy your day." He crawls back into the box long before the bell rings.

FARLEY DECIDED to visit Dr. Nichols rather than get the news on the telephone. He drove the Toyota around the red mountain toward the center of St. George. Gas stations, motels, family restaurants, small shopping centers, a hardware store, a McDonald's, a Taco Bell, a Burger King, a Dunkin' DoNuts, a Weinershnitzel, a Mormon temple, a Carl's Jr., a Pizza Hut, an A&W Root Beer, two large grocery stores, real estate offices, chiropractors, doctors, dentist offices, Dixie Junior College, the high school, the grammar school, Brigham Young's home, condominiums, houses—mostly white, car lots, a Mexican restaurant, a golf course, three tire stores, a garage, chapels, another garage, more motels and more family restaurants. This was what had been built in this corner of the southwestern American desert. Brigham Young had sent a troop of men and women to settle the area a hundred or so years before. This was what civilization had brought to the land, Farley mused as he turned off St. George Boulevard onto Third Street where Dr. Nichols' office occupied the South 352 space. He parked on the street next to a large gutter across from the cemetery. The gutter, he thought, collected the rains from the desert storms—and the cemetery, garbage dump, and car dump collected the rest.

The office interior was painted a soft shade of pink. Dr. Nichols' secretary wore a lovely pink blouse. She politely pointed Farley to the waiting room. He thought of lifting a magazine, but didn't. He looked at the *Book of Mormon* on the corner table and at a nicely framed photograph on the wall in front of him. It was a vertical shot of a cloud in a white-blue sky. Beams of tender light slipped through the upper and lower edges of the cloud giving the viewer a sense of the supernatural. Farley tried to imagine what the supernatural might really look like. He thought nature and being were the same thing, so super nature would be equivalent to super being which would be hard to imagine except for a super mind which made him think of Superman who was a very natural Hollywood actor with very natural props and cameras to help him fly and a very natural girlfriend who loved him deeply on camera. Dr. Nichols rescued him from his reverie.

"Mr. Farley," he said as if punctuating the name with a thin question mark.

"Yes," Farley said rising to shake hands.

"Come on into my office. It's good of you to come. Your mother's told me about you." They entered the office where Farley took the standard seat in the chair, not leather here, across from the doctor's desk. The doctor wasted no time in looking Farley in the eye to say, "It's not good news, but it could be worse. She shows all the symptoms of Alzheimer's. I assume you are familiar with it."

"A little," Farley said.

"Well, it used to be called senility, but now we've zeroed in a little on the problem and one strain of it is Alzheimer's. It means her mind is unable to recall current information. She is able to remember things that happened before the disease took root, but new information doesn't record."

"I had observed as much," Farley said.

"Did she remember you?" Dr. Nichols asked.

"She asked me if I'd brought my golf clubs, so I guess she did. However sometimes I think she confuses me with my brother."

"Where does he live?"

"In Florida."

"Well, that's typical. She will confuse things like who is in the room with her and who is coming or going, but she does have a sense of who you are from the deeper past."

"I guess there's not much to be done about it," Farley said.

"Not much medically speaking. It's important to try to keep her in her normal surroundings as long as possible. Radical changes seem to make things worse."

"I suspect she really shouldn't be living alone, should she?"

"The truth is her condition deteriorated rather rapidly. I saw her twice over a three-month period for other problems. The first visit I really detected nothing serious, but by the second visit—ten days ago—she manifested all the symptoms of Alzheimer's. I told her to call you to have you call me as soon as possible, which I presume she did." Dr. Nichols glanced at the photograph on the wall to his right which was also a cloud shot.

"Did you take the pictures, Doctor?"

"In fact, I did. You're only the second person to have guessed. Are you a photographer?" he asked as if seeking a moment's rest from disease.

"No, I haven't taken a picture since my second child was born. Actually, mother called me but didn't tell me to call you. When I heard her on the phone, I decided I better come out."

"It's a good thing you did. She shouldn't be alone. Are you able to stay with her for awhile?"

"Normally no, but I'm on a sabbatical year so I can."

"That's fortunate. However, if things get worse she might need 24-hour care. We'll wait and see." (*Things*, Farley thought, trying to imagine the inside of his mother's brain as a tinker toy or a wrench or a coffee cup.)

"When should I get back to you?" Farley asked.

"Let's say in another ten days give me a call."

"Can I leave her for any length of time?" he asked, thinking of the golf course outside her window.

"A couple hours at the most. Be sure to tell her clearly where you're going and when you'll be back. She won't remember, but all reassurances help."

"Will do," Farley said, feeling he'd heard enough. He stood and extended his hand across the desk. He stepped out of the room, told the secretary she had a nice blouse, and got in nine holes before the sun went down.

∂

NEW YORK TIMES Service: John Noble Wilford

Galaxy Sixty Times
the Size of Milky Way

Astronomers have identified what they think is the largest galaxy ever observed, more than sixty times the size of the Milky Way. They believe that in its tremendous mass they may find clues to forces responsible for the clustering of matter in the universe.

The galaxy, comprising more than 100 trillion stars, is the extremely bright object at the center of a rich cluster of galaxies known as Abell 2029.

Analysis of new telescopic images indicates that the object is a distinct galaxy more than 6 million light years in diameter, scientists report in the issue of the journal *Science* published Friday.

(Does the universe know when Friday is? Farley thinks as he reads.)

Until now, the largest known galaxy was Markarian 348, which is about 1.3 million light years wide. The Milky Way, Earth's home galaxy, is about 100,000 light years across. A light year, the distance that a beam of light moving at 186,000 miles a second will travel in a year, is roughly 6 trillion miles.

New York Times Service: John Noble Wilford

The Big Bang Theory
has a Black Hole

A critical element of the widely accepted Big Bang theory about the origin and evolution of the universe is being discarded by some of its staunchest advocates, which has thrown the field of cosmology into turmoil.

According to the Big Bang theory, matter from the explosive moment of cosmic creation...

(What keeps them believing in a creation? Farley thinks.)

...originally was evenly spread throughout the universe.

But galaxies tend to be clumped together, an awkward fact that astronomers have sought to explain by assuming that cold, invisible matter is a major attractive force.

The cold dark matter model, as it is called, accounts well for local clustering but does not explain the giant superstructures recently found in galactic surveys, such as the 'great wall,' a string of galaxies stretching across the sky for at least a half-billion light-years.

A new analysis of a highly accurate...

(What is accurate for man may not be accurate for the universe, Farley thinks.)

...survey conducted by the Infrared Astronomical Satellite now shows the universe to be full of such superstructures and companion supervoids.

(Are superstructures, supervoids, superman and supernaturals born of the same mother? Farley wonders)

A major problem is that these structures appear to be far too vast to have formed since the Big Bang.

Farley went into the supermarket for taco mix. He walked past the pancake and waffle boxes, then bumped into the block of cold cereal packages. As a child he had consumed innumerable cartons of Tony-the-Tiger's Frosted Flakes, but he had not bought any for years. His breakfasts had long since been reduced to bread, butter, jam, coffee and orange juice. Farley had missed the evolution in cold cereal.

He stood in front of the cereals and turned his head left and right. He figured it was a three-point shot from one end of the section to the other. In thirty years the Frosted Flakes, Corn Flakes, Cherrios, Raisin Bran and Wheaties had spawned all this. He saw Crunches, Krinkles, Loops, Krunches, Crinkles, Crisps, Trix, Puffs, Vampires, Ghostbusters, and Pops with interchangeable candy, fruit and marshmallow labels. The light browns, beiges and cream colors had turned green, purple, pink, yellow, bright orange and chocolate brown. The eye, he thought, is a delicious target.

Before counting the varieties, he had estimated about sixty. He passed sixty before he had fingered half the shelf. There were exactly one hundred and forty-nine cold cereals to choose from. Was this somehow in connection with the Big Bang? Had the same happened in peanut butter, Jello, and cake mixes? He was certain it had, though he felt no need to verify. He found the tacos and was not surprised to see that they too had taken on new forms and that the packages were no longer uniquely yellow with red and brown trim. This had happened in less than a year. He was reasonably sure he had last bought taco mix six to eight months before. But perhaps then he had been blind to the evolution. Perhaps he had grabbed his standard brand mechanically as he turned his cart to the cheeses. He would never know and he couldn't remember a thing about the last time he bought tacos. We cannot remember 99.9% of what we do, he thought with a joyful tingle as he revved up the cart and powered it to the open refrigerator that housed the great galaxy of canned and bottled beer. Here too the bang had banged.

"It's me, Mom," Farley said around the grocery bag cupped in his right arm.

"Who?"

"It's me, Larry."

"Oh, Larry. Hi. Where are the children?"

"They're in California, Mom. They've still got school."

"When will they be coming?"

"End of June when school's out. I'll probably have Carole put them on a plane to Las Vegas."

"Is Carole here?"

"No, she's with the children in Moraga."

"Is she coming tomorrow then?"

"No, I don't think she'll make it out this summer. Just the kids."

"Oh. I was just making a cottage cheese salad. Would you like a bite?"

"Thanks, but I've got my heart set on tacos. Would you like one?"

"Thanks, Larry, but I'm not doing so well with spicy food any more. I'll just have some cottage cheese. Would you like some?"

"No thanks, Mom. I'll have some tacos."

"Did you play golf this morning?"

"Nah, just went to the store. Maybe I'll hit a few this afternoon."

"Larry, have you seen the car? I went out to the garage this morning and it wasn't there."

"We sold it last week, Mom. We decided you shouldn't drive now."

"Oh, we did. Who bought it?"

"The dealer over on St. George Boulevard."

"How much was it?"

"He gave us three thousand which seemed reasonable from a dealer."

"Oh, that's good."

"We put the money in your account."

"We'll need it for a new one probably."

"We won't be needing a new one soon. My car is plenty."

Farley stared at Freda in a curl on the kitchen floor. He wondered how many light years there were across the galaxies inside her skull. Then he turned to his mother who sat at the table and was forking her food toward the tongue that lay limply on her lower lip. Bang, bang, he thought, thinking of the 100 trillion stars in Abell 2029 and then of the 100 trillion stars that made up his mother who went by the similar name of Adell.

ᴣᵔ

From THE LETTER it was hard to tell who had pulled the hit and run. Had his wife filled her bag, then grabbed the goods and run? Or had the agronomist sowed his sack of seed, then wandered off in search of new arable land? They hadn't lasted until Easter. Four months wouldn't get them into love's hall of fame, Farley mused. In any case, his wife explained things thus:

April 8

Farley,

I'm writing—instead of calling—because of late I've had a terrible aversion to all forms of modern communication, i.e. television, telephone, etc. Adoula spent so much time zonked in front of the tube I thought the thing would blow up, which unfortunately it didn't. Never did I realize how much crap was squeezed through that screen until I watched it through his eyes. I had suggested it to be a means to his acquisition of the English language, but it ended up pushing his I.Q. toward the single digit. Man has to be the lowest common denominator of existence if TV is taken into consideration. And how many channels have we got now?

Anyway—as you might have guessed—we bang banged until we blew the house down and until he got hooked on "Leave It To Beaver." Next time I'll put a clause in the concubinal contract limiting TV to twenty minutes a day. I mean "Championship Bowling" and "Big Time Wrestling"! Give a brain a break! When he started recording "Father Knows Best" reruns and watching them more than twice, I knew the curtain was down.

Who can I tell this to but you? Pitter patter.

Needless to say, I'm sorry about your mother's condition which is just another example of what I've said for years: Life is a game for losers. What in hell did she do to deserve this?

Obviously nothing, which is exactly the point. In 90 years they'll
have a cool cure for Alzheimer's which will mean that man will
have to find a new way to rot. How can you take watching her
slowly wilt away? But then what can't you take?

I'm almost ashamed to say that I've actually missed Freda
and her bi-weekly vomit on the carpet. At least she never turned
on the TV. Has she caught any rattlesnakes out there in that rusty
dust?

You should call the kids more often as they talk and ask
about you more than I would have expected. I guess if nothing
else you were—are—a good father. As for husband, the verdict
is still out. I never knew if I married a man or an idea, even
though when the man manifested he wasn't unmanly.

What's it been? Four months? Can you still hit a golf ball
straight?

Yours unruly,
Carole

P.S. If I write again I might throw the meat out of the cave
and explain the why of the je-je-jealousy crises of this fast
dying sparrow. That is, if anybody is still interested.

More banging, Farley thought as he put down the letter. And he
remembered why he had married his wife. Anything beats boredom.

He called upstairs to his mother in her bedroom. She answered,
asking him for help. He found her spread across the bed with an
arm and a leg through the sleeves of a blouse. The telephone was
off the hook dangling from the night table.

"I was trying to get dressed and to call Carl in Florida," she
said with what he detected to be a twinge of embarrassment.

"Let's get you straightened out here," he said, "then we can
call Carl." As he freed her from the blouse he tried to pin a number
to the times she had dressed and undressed her two sons. A couple
thousand at least, he thought. He sat beside her on the bed, held

open the blouse, and re-threaded her arms through the sleeves. Then she pulled her elbows to her side and sat hunched and still, her bare legs floating parallel on the wrinkled blue bedspread. Where is she? Farley thought, knowing that the thought was not a question for the question could never be answered for anyone any time in any circumstances. Bless her with peace, he thought addressing no one and nothing except the habit of well-wishing. Shit, he said no louder that a thought, and he put his arm on the back of her neck and set his hand on her shoulder.

"Where's Artie?" she asked. Artie had been Farley's father and her husband. "Oh wait," she said, softly sparing Farley the need to answer.

Where is she? he thought, thinking you can't get to infinity with road signs. He dressed her in her maroon slacks, then dialed his brother in Florida and got no answer.

"Would you like to watch a little TV?" he suggested, trying to take her thinking away from her failure to dress herself, though such might have already been the case.

"I was getting ready for Carl," she said.

"He won't be coming just now, Mom, so why don't we see if 'I Love Lucy' is on?"

"When is he coming?"

"I'm not sure. We'll try to call him later."

"Will he bring the children?"

"He doesn't have any children, Mom."

"Oh."

"My kids will be here in a couple months. As soon as they're out of school."

"Oh, Larry's children."

"Yes."

Farley escorted his mother downstairs and flipped on the TV. She sat on the couch and again drew her elbows to her side and stared in the direction of the yakking machine like a frozen avalanche victim might look into the rubble of a razed home. Farley found Lucy, kissed his mother near the eye, then headed for the nine-hole course at the north end of town.

DEAR CAROLE,

Your letter came as a good dessert after a bad dinner, that is, something that made sense to gustatory cells used to caviar and bubbly wine. Other than Mom's doctor and the guy at the Pro Shop, I've talked to no one lately that speaks out of the same microphone. Mother is an angel, as always, but one who has left the world of nouns, verbs, and adjectives glued to every day experience. I love her, enjoy her, tend her, play golf enough, drink wine bought like a criminal from State Liquor Stores, smoke, walk Freda in that rusty dust, and watch the sky paint better things than I ever could. But I don't get much normal conversation. Hence your letter spoke to a famished brain. Confess, I must, that I don't not enjoy it. The hunger that is. The lack of language that is. The shared garbage pails that is. Social beasts we are, but little by little the social can probably be beaten from the beast. Why am I answering you? You know what I think of any *why* question, but for high school's sake let's say I wanted to sit at mother's unused typewriter. In the past a typewriter has served me well as crucifix, candle, and lifesaving vest. Need is a glorious thing.

You politely left open the verdict on my merit as a husband. Let me punch in a few words about yours as a wife. The other day while roaming with Freda through a lovely place called Snow Canyon (we should buy a house or tent there if nuclear fusion ever occurs), I had a profound revelation: women may be divided into two categories—those you want to continue to sniff after copulation and those that make you feel like you've just masturbated. You, dreadful darling, are among the former. For this nature was good to me. There must be thousands of sad souls who marry women of the second category—for themselves, that is—out of some kind of coupling desperation.

I think, therefore I am. Descartes.

I am, therefore I type. Farley.

As you are sorry about my mother, I am dismayed for the

agronomist. Had he only chosen Stockholm for his doctorate he might have been spared the brain-chewing anesthesia of American TV. However, I might say it's kept mother close to her feet. I've noticed if I forget to sit her in front of the Lucy Show, the rest of the day is tougher, at least for her. She, as you said, deserves nothing of what inflicts her, but other than a couple times when she's said "I know something's wrong," I'm not sure she is in a bad state. I mean she doesn't seem to suffer. Her wild nouns and verbs don't fly back and knock her out. Her friends are few and understanding. The doctor is not an unkind man. She sleeps poorly, but that's nothing new. Her diet is still bird-like, but that also goes back to my childhood at least. I've heard a bit about this so-called Alzheimer's disease, but I've yet to hear anyone say it might simply be nature's way of cushioning decay. That Mom makes no sense of the present, recent past, and future might be a good thing. For rolling toward the grave she is. Aren't we all, you say, but some of us are closer than others. I love to think of death as other than the opposite of life, but sometimes I wonder if the two are maybe the only real poles in the circus tent. I wonder. Do we—can we—do any more than wonder?

Pitter patter, as you said.

Pitter patter, donc je suis.

Revelation II. This one received while pulling a seven iron from bag and looking up ninth fairway toward the clubhouse that makes delicious bacon and tomato sandwiches: A woman can be judged by how she would look if presented on a menu. The more of her you would want to eat, the greater the amour. Where there is love, there are taste buds. Before slapping the seven-iron, I peered into the crackling Utah sky and quickly ran through the list of the women in my life. Only you—it was decided—would I happily consume grilled from neck to ankle. I confess your toes left me appetiteless, but with a wine sauce I could probably get them down as well. Why am I telling you this? To make you feel wanted. Which you are. Which you want to be. Might being wanted be the tale of humanity? And would not what is truly wanted pass for food. By the time I got to the green, which I three-putted cheerfully, I had added Ricky and

Rosanne to my list of delicacies. But they are not in competition with your spicy curves.

Had you junked the TV, I would have said nothing. Better to watch the desert sky.

Yours culinarily,
Fricasseed Farley

$\sim$

WE SEE FARLEY arriving early to class. He has a load of blankets under one arm and a portable globe of the world in the opposite hand. When he lays the blankets on the desk, we notice that there is a black book in the pile. He places the globe on the pulpit and gives it a gentle spin. He reaches with his left hand into the side pocket of his herringbone sport coat and removes a box of thumbtacks. We then watch as he climbs on various chairs and desks to cover the windows with the blankets. The room is now semi-dark, dark enough for his purposes. To read he will need the small flashlight that he has in an inside jacket pocket.

There is a bell followed by the protoplasmic trickle of students who show little sign of surprise at the state of the room. We hear a second bell and we see Farley sit at the desk facing the flock. He switches on the flashlight, opens the black book, and begins to read. His tone is not solemn as might be expected, but rather he speaks like a sportscaster doing a basketball game on the radio:

> "Innn the bee-ginning Gawd crrree-ated heaven and earth. And the earth was vvvoid and empty, and daarkness was upon the face of the deep; and thhhe spirit of Gaawd moved over the waa-ters. And Gaawd saaaid: Be light made. And light was maaade."

The students now watch Farley go over to the door and turn on the two light switches. He returns to the desk and picks up the book, then goes to the pulpit and stands behind the globe. He reads (faster this time):

> "Gaawd also said: Let the waters that are under the heaven be gathered together into wunnnn place, and let the dry land

106

appeeere. And it was so done. And Gawd called the dry land,
Earth; and the gathering together of the waters he called Seas.
And Gawd saw that it was gooooooooooood."

Farley lifts the globe with his left hand, spins it with a flip of
the right, then walks around and around the class in an elliptical
pattern. We have heard some of the students laugh at their teacher's
radio voice. Now we hear them laugh again as he speaks (this time
in a normal voice) while continuing to circle the room:

"And then He created the little fish and the big fish and the creep-
ing creatures and the flying ones and then the walking ones and
then—ladies and gentlemen—He created us, male and female
alike, and not alike. Then he took a time out, pulled
himself out of the game and watched beavers create dams and
birds nests and Eskimos igloos and Indians tepees and Ray Kroc
McDonald's restaurants and Venetians Venice and New
Yorkers very tall buildings and Polynesians hula dancing and
Michelangelo the Sistine Chapel and Clint Eastwood the
unshaved look and Germans the Volkswagen and Americans the
'All men are created equal' and the Chinese acupuncture and
Mexicans excellent tortillas and Americans cars and Americans
car accidents and Bach the Brandenburg Concertos and cowboys
branding irons and cats the meow and Marcel Marceau the mime
and Moslems the mosque and Ming T'ai Tsu the Ming dynasty
and Midas the muffler and Magic Johnson the triple double and
Morse the code and Moses the Mosaic Law and men and women
meat loaf and Mesopotamia and martinis and money and mus-
tard and mohair sweaters and midnight mass and maple syrup."

Farley and the globe stop their rotations. He sits on the desk in
front of the class, puts down the world and for a minute says nothing.
Then, "So...what about a metaphysics that includes the notion of
creation? Can we conceive of being without thinking there was *A
Creation*? Have you ever imagined the possibility that being was

not created, that it always has been, that when Einstein said that matter could neither be created nor destroyed he wasn't just whistling Dixie? Might the concept *creation* be but a small pop in the human head that satisfies the great big human desire to make sense out of the eternal nonsensical? Imagine for a moment the possibility that being is infinite, that it has always been, that nothing was created but that being only becomes—that is, changes—at least for the human eye and heart—and that all being is inextricably tied together forever and forever. But to do this you must imagine that the Eskimo and the igloo are one and that the cat and the meow cannot be separated."

Farley wonders if he has gone too far too fast, but he doesn't care. He is enjoying himself. He excuses himself for a drink of water. We see the students in various states of fidgeting, speaking, and what appears to be reflection or fatigue.

FARLEY LIKED Vladimer Horowitz, but he was hard to listen to while he looked at his mother. He had bought a cassette called *The Last Recording* at the big drugstore on St. George Boulevard. The tape might have been a delivery mistake for it looked lonely amid the Crystal Gayles, Glen Campbells, Waylon Jennings, and the rest of the cicatricial cowboy tunes. But it was there, he took it, and Horowitz—now dead—was into Isolde's *Liebestod*, created dually by Richard Wagner and Franz Liszt. His mother was stroking Freda, the two of them on her canary-yellow couch. Dog hairs meant nothing to her now. She was calling Freda *Rex*, the name given to the German shepherd of Farley's youth that had bit the paper boy and been summarily put to sleep.

Art Farley had whisked Rex off to the vet's while his oldest son, then twelve, was winging curveballs at baffled little leaguers who were only used to the straight stuff. Farley came home with the strikeout record—twelve in the maximum four innings—only to learn that sporting exploits lose their luster when the rest of life is ugly. Rex was dead; his house and life were empty for weeks to come.

"Good doggie, Rex. You're just a good doggie," his mother said as Horowitz leaped on to the musical simulation of climax. Farley watched his mother's vein-drenched hand reach under Freda's neck. The dog groaned with joy and she said, "Good doggie, Rex."

The cassette stopped and the room filled with the hum of the dated tape machine. Farley saw Tristan sniffing Isolde's mane and his mother lowering her nose between Freda's ears. "Would you like to go to the Sizzler for lunch?" he asked.

"I'd love to, Larry. They have a wonderful salad bar."

"You used to go there a lot, didn't you?"

"Yes. I always have a salad and a Coke. Your father has the steak and lobster."

"Maybe I'll have it," Farley said.

"Do you want breakfast first?"

"We had that, Mom. I'll take Freda out for a few minutes and then we'll go. How's that?"

"Fine, Larry. Will Carl be here before we leave?"

"We don't know when he's coming yet. He said he had a few things to tie up before he could come."

"Oh, he did." It was half question, half answer. Farley grabbed the leash from the door handle and Freda jumped off the couch and began pawing at his legs. "Where are you going?" his mother asked.

"I'll just take Freda for a little walk, then we'll go to the Sizzler."

"When will we go?"

"About a half hour, Mom."

"Fine, Larry."

Man and dog walked south past the golf course to the end of Bloomington development. Here paved roads became dirt and the land was grey-brown. Freda was loosed from the leash and began slaloming through sagebrush. She caught scent of a desert taupe, chased it to its hole, and began digging furiously. Digging at death's doorstep, thought Farley. Then he thought, For Freda, nothing of the kind. Around his dog's head the earth turned to a halo of dust. Then the digging stopped and Freda sauntered back with the taupe snug between her jaws. She stopped at a spot that was somewhere beyond good and evil and let the warm little body fall in front of her master's feet. One of Farley's jewels, he thought genuflecting, and for a moment he watched death glisten in the light of noon.

"Mother, you're eating your napkin." She was. Fortunately it was paper. Had she not been taking large bites, Farley might have let her have it with her dessert.

"Oh sorry," she said. "I am." She slowly gathered her fingers in a bunch and started withdrawing red strands from her mouth. Farley looked for signs of embarrassment, but wasn't sure if there were any. "Did you enjoy your steak and lobster, dear?" she asked with her tongue not fully set for speech.

"The steak was better than the lobster this time."

"Oh," she said.

"Do you want to eat your ice cream?" he asked.

"My ice cream," she said. "Haven't they brought it yet?"

"It's beside your napkin, Mom. Why don't you have a little and we'll be on our way."

"My napkin is torn," she said.

"It is," he said.

So LET'S ASK a simple question: Which makes more sense, a universe that was created or a universe that has always been?"

After Farley excused himself for a drink, David has tried to understand why his teacher has read Genesis as if commentating a basketball game. He has correctly guessed that the intention was to get the students to think twice about a concept that is more or less tattooed on their brains.

"Actually, until today, I had never conceived of the possibility that life was not created," he says. "But with a little thought it might make more sense to believe that being always was."

"Anybody else?"

"I don't know, sir, but if God or somebody like Him didn't put the show on the stage, who did?"

"Well, Max," Farley says, "your question reveals exactly the problem we're trying to get at. We have a lot of difficulty imagining that the show was never put on stage. We see life as a series of beginnings and ends—things get made, used up, and discarded—plants grow from seeds, then die and are never heard from again. This is how we see it. But let's think...did the seed really come from nowhere? No, it and the conditions for growth were already there in some form. And when the plant dies we may not see it anymore, but the remains are crushed back into the ground or mixed with dust. Indeed they are somewhere. We might see beginning and end, but are we seeing correctly?"

"I don't know," Max says. "But what about with people?"

"Looks the same to me," David says immediately. "We see sperm and egg and think that's the beginning, but what made the sperm and the egg? And what made what made them? And so on back to infinity. And then we see death as an end, but who's to say? The body we see goes into the ground or gets burned and we can't see it anymore, but that doesn't mean it's at an end."

Farley thinks the boy will be a teacher if his thinking can get the best of his thinking. "You took the words out of my mouth, David," he says. "What we see here is that our way of breaking down reality will probably determine our way of answering the question about creation. If we chop reality into bits and pieces, then we'll get beginnings and ends and such. But if we see being as a big whole—that is whole with a 'w'—then creation might look different. We can imagine a great continuous flux that may change for the human eye, but really reaches to the depths and sides and ins and outs of infinity."

Christine Lasenger feels fear, fear like she remembers when she saw "Psycho" the first time. But then, for once, she stops and asks herself what is she really afraid of. The fear returns before she is able to answer.

Arthur Windell looks at his watch. It is a quarter to twelve.

Elizabeth again thinks of the American Indian. She also thinks maybe Farley hasn't shaved since the day before yesterday.

David's hand is up again.

"David."

"If nothing was created, that means everything always was, which means everything probably always will be, but the word 'every-THING' is the wrong word, isn't it?"

"Isn't it?" Farley says. "And...?"

"No, that's all," David says.

"Anybody else?" Farley asks.

Nobody else.

The students leave and we see the teacher climb back on the desks and chairs to remove the hanging blankets. He folds them, opens a window and lights a cigarette.

ॐ

DEAR FARLEY,

I said I'd get to the jealousy stuff, but let's not get to it—let's start with it. If you've taught me one thing it's that we never really get at causes. (In spite of what you might think, I really wasn't a bad student.) I got the message when you used to growl at all my theories of child-rearing—we never really know why they turn out the way they do. Okay, we don't. Professor Farley would then extrapolate to declare the same for the origins of wife's jealousy. Wife agrees. Now what? I think (Professor Farley would stop me and say there is no *I* that thinks but only some mysterious activity calling thinking, but what the hell, you've got to say something. Do you? the Professor says.) that having experienced said emotion hundreds of times, I know enough to say that it was stronger than I. (There's no *I* the Professor repeats, only a continuous unending being that interacts with the rest of being.) *I* felt—after profound empirical study—that the feeling always came in spite of all efforts to stop it. And what's more, I've decided jealousy was never—is never—a sign of love, but rather a sign of a lack of it. The jealous one does not love, cannot love, because the object of the love gets lost and clouded by the emotion. The eyes of jealousy distort the picture such that the picture is not seen. Hence I have never loved you or any other. I now think that the only feelings I've ever had for a male were something closer to water being thrown on a campfire: I was the fire, the need was burning, and I used the man to put it out. Need of what? Need of yin for yang, I guess. This does not mean I didn't prefer some over others—I mean I did marry you instead of one of the forty-seven other ducks that came quacking at my cage—but it wasn't love that was greater for you and a couple others. It was just that you were more wood for a bigger fire. And let's face it from another angle: how can anybody say they love somebody when they don't want the best for the other person, but only want the other person to do certain things for them. I wanted you for me alone thinking nothing of what you might want or need for you. Love? I'd call it unadulterated *gimme.* Use the other to screw the mirror to the wall. So far the only trace of love I've noticed on the planet is a few parents for their children. Here I've seen a few who really seem to want what the child wants. But even here we might slip into a murky sea.

Since Adoula hit the road I've put things into a little perspective (perspective: what man lacks most, the Professor says with great humility.) I see myself as some kind of cute hole in the middle of a cemetery that is waiting to be filled with a coffin with me in it (unfortunately), but the hole will always be too big for the little coffin. In other words, I ain't what I used to think I was. Let's just say the jealousy was a birth defect, a pus-filled pimple that wouldn't go away. Sorry so much juice splattered on you.

Have I so far said less than nothing, Professor? You were fun to walk around the reservoir with as long as we didn't meet any beautiful busty ghosts. The kids still hold you heavenly in their hearts. Rosanne can count to five in French, German and Italian. Ricky thinks he's a cross between Bubba Smith and Zorro.

Creamed Carole

P.S. Re-read letter. Thought more was there than is. What have I left out? I could have said something about the possibility of my being cured. What have I put in? What came out? Does it matter before or after you've pulled a five-iron from your golf bag?

DEAR CAROLE,

Does life have a goal? (Sorry. I have no students these days, Freda doesn't care, and my mother couldn't if she wanted to. So you get the June 6, eleven o'clock lecture.) I voted no as I was lining up a tricky putt on the third hole at Bloomington yesterday. Playing by myself as always, I wondered if anybody actually cared if I rolled in this eight-footer or not. Is there any mechanism in the universe that has established if this putt should or should not fall into the cup? No, thought I, as I stroked the ball squarely in the middle to save bogey.

Does life have a goal? Does it strive to be anything? Men want things, but so do rabbits and squirrels and rain clouds and flowers. But is the whole of being striving to become anything? No, I voted, as I strutted rabbit-with-full-stomach-like to the fourth tee.

A billion individual goals do not make up a goal for the whole. But hasn't man always assumed that since he wants something, the universe must want something too. Because he is headed to the supermarket he presumes being is headed there too. Error of errors. Drrrriiinngggggg. Have a good weekend. The bell has rescued the uninterested.

Mother is worse. I haven't called the doctor yet but will. I think my call will be equivalent to packing her into a home where her disintegration will be properly surveyed by a group of underpaid nurses. Before she was able to answer a question. Now she cannot remember the question long enough to answer it. I, however, have retained your last letter long enough to say that Professor Farley loved your theory of love and briefly caught a glimpse of an empty coffin being axed and used for fire wood.

Tell the kids their daddy loves them.

f.

$\backsim$

M OM, I JUST talked with the doctor and he wants us to come see him tomorrow."

"Oh, didn't we see him yesterday?"

"No, you haven't been there in almost a month."

"I think maybe he should be here when your children arrive. I'm sure they'd get along so well together."

"They won't be here for a couple more weeks."

"How old is he now? Didn't he just have his tenth birthday?"

"That was your cousin Claris' boy. They stopped by last week on their way down to Phoenix."

"Well, they do get along fine when then play together just like you and Bill Milton used to."

"Yes, we did."

"I'll have to get ready then. I haven't seen Claris since her husband died."

"He asked us to come tomorrow morning, Mom. Would you like a cup of coffee?"

"She said she thinks she might move here for the climate."

"She moved to Phoenix last week."

"Should I wear anything special?"

"How about a cup of coffee and some toast?"

"Our neighbors said they'd probably be moving back to Los Angeles because he was out of work so Claris could move in their place and then he could play with the Milton boy more often."

"I'll get you some coffee, Mom."

"If you think it's a good idea, but I think maybe I should get dressed first because I wouldn't want them to come without us being ready. I'll have to go to the store before we have breakfast then."

"Let's see if Lucy's on." Farley turned on the television and his mother, though dressed, headed upstairs to dress again. Farley called her back but she said she needed to put on something appropriate for when they got here. He didn't argue.

When she came back downstairs she had not changed clothes, but had the telephone book in her hand. "I can't find the doctor's number," she said.

"It's all right, Mom. I talked to him a few minutes ago. We'll see him tomorrow."

"Will we have time before Claris comes?"

"We will. Here's a cup of coffee for you."

"Thank you, Larry. I think I'll watch TV for awhile before Claris comes. Then we can all go to the doctor together. I think they'll get along fine."

Farley watched his mother watching television. Her eyelids reminded him of deflated basketballs. He imagined the connection of eye to brain to heart, of ear to brain to heart to eye to tongue to belly to brain. He saw science dissecting, trying to find beginnings and ends where there were none. One does not dissect a mother, he thought. One smells her. One watches her. He watched her watching, wondering where a kiss on the forehead would wander. Then he walked to her and kissed her and she said nothing. He went to the kitchen to prepare toast. She took the channel selector and held it in her upturned left palm as one would hold a small mouse. She pulled it near to her chest, lowered her eyes, and with her right index began pecking at the numbers. She settled on a morning children's show that featured the standard providential virgin entertaining a room full of nearly self-conscious pre-schoolers. Setting the toast on the coffee table, Farley noticed that the virgins didn't look as virginal as they used to. This one, as she clomped round the room, had a hip motion that reminded him of the churning of the locomotive apparatus on the front wheels of his first electric train. Farley thought she must have been using the kiddie show as a stepping stone toward a career in Hollywood.

"Thank you for the toast, Larry," his mother said.

"Would you like me to see if there's anything else on?" he offered, gently lifting the little mouse from her hand.

"No. I think that's Carl's son on TV there."

"You mean Ricky. Carl doesn't have any children." The virgin had herded the group into a circle and they were singing, *The itsy bitsy spider crawled up the water spout. Down came the rain and washed the spider out...* The first phrase had them raising their hands over their heads; with the second they dropped them and wiggled their fingers to simulate rain. The children's fingers seemed bent on doing the spider in; the virgin's, Farley thought, were wanting to tickle.

"He has a boy and a girl," Adell Farley said. "They'll be coming this summer."

"I'm looking forward to it," Farley said. His mother took back the mouse and punched a finger into its eye. Farley pondered the circuit, forever closed, running from eye to brain to finger to mouse to screen to performers to camera to screen to eye to heart to brain to finger. While he pondered, she poked. The virgin and her flock came and went, came and went. Like the stars, thought Farley, like the stars. One of which the snappy virgin was trying to become.

"YOU REMEMBER not long ago when we discussed the problem of thinking," Farley does not ask, but says. "We talked about what thinking might be, where it originates, if thinking is thought or if thinking is something that imposes itself on beings like ourselves. Let's keep these notions in mind while I read you a passage about consciousness. It will take a few minutes, but try to hold what you hear in your delicate little noggins."

The students look as alert as the teacher can hope for, so he begins:

> *"Of the 'genius of the species.'* The problem of consciousness (more correctly: of becoming conscious of oneself) steps before us only when we begin to understand to what extent we could do without it: and we are now placed at this beginning of understanding by physiology and the natural history of the animals. For we could think, feel, will, recollect, we could likewise *act* in every sense of the word—and yet none of this would need to 'enter into our consciousness' (as one says in a metaphor). The whole of life would be possible without, as it were, regarding itself in a mirror; as indeed, in our case, by far the greater part of this life even now does pass without this reflection—including our thinking, feeling, willing life, however offensive it may sound to a philosopher of earlier days. To *what end* consciousness at all, if it is in the main superfluous? Now it seems to me that refinement and strength of consciousness always stands in proportion to the capacity for communication of a human being (or animal), capacity for communication in turn in proportion to the need for communication. Supposing this observation to be correct, I may then go on to conjecture that consciousness evolved at all only under the pressure of the need for communication—that it was from the very first necessary and useful only between man and man (between commanders and obeyers in particular) and also evolved only in proportion to the degree

of this usefulness. Consciousness is really only a connecting network between man and man—only as such did it have to evolve: the solitary and predatory man would not have needed it. That our actions, thoughts, feelings, movements come into our consciousness—at least part of them—is the consequence of a fearfully protracted compulsion which lay over man: as the most endangered animal he *required* help, protection, he required his own kind. He had to express his needs, know how to make himself understood—and for all that, he first had need of consciousness, that is to say, he himself needs to know what he lacks, to know how he feels, to know what he is thinking. For, to say it again: man, like every living creature, thinks continually but does not know it; thinking which has become conscious is only the smallest part of it—let us say the most superficial part, the worst part. For only this conscious thinking takes place in words, that is to say in communication-signs, by which the origin of consciousness reveals itself.

"In short, the evolution of language and the evolution of consciousness (*not* of reason but only of reason's becoming conscious of itself) go hand in hand. Add to this the fact that it is not only language which serves as a bridge between man and man, but the glance, the clasp, the bearing do so, too; our becoming-conscious of our own sense-impressions, the power of fixing them and, as it were, setting them outside ourselves, has increased in the measure that the need grew to transmit them to others by signs. The sign-inventing man is at the same time the man who is ever more sharply conscious of himself; only as a social animal did man learn to become conscious of himself. He does it still, he does it more and more.

"My idea, as one can see, is that consciousness does not really belong to the existence of man as an individual but rather to that in him which is community and herd; that, as follows from this, it has also evolved in refinement only with regard to usefulness for community and herd, and that consequently each of us, even with the best will to understand himself in as individual a way as possible, 'to know himself,' will nonetheless bring into his consciousness only what is not individual in him, his 'average'—that our thought itself is continually, as it were, outvoted by the character of consciousness, by the 'genius of the species' which rules in it—and translated back into the perspective of the herd. Our actions are fundamentally one and all in an incomparable way personal, unique, boundlessly individual, there is no doubt about that. But as soon as we translate them into consciousness, they no longer seem to be. This is the essence of phenomenalism and perspectivism as I understand them: Owing to the nature of animal consciousness, the world of which we can become conscious is only a surface— and sign-world, a world made universal and common—and that everything which becomes conscious thereby becomes shallow, thin, relatively stupid, general, sign, characteristic of the herd; all becoming-conscious involves a great fundamental corruption, falsification, superficializing, and generalization. Ultimately, the growth of consciousness becomes a danger; and he who lives among the most conscious Europeans even knows that it is a disease. You will guess that it is not the opposition of subject and object that concerns me here: this distinction I leave to the epistemologists who have become entangled in the snares of grammar (the metaphysics of the people). It is even less the opposition of 'thing-in-itself' and appearance; for we do not know nearly enough to be entitled to any such distinction. For we have no organ at all for knowledge, for truth: we know (or believe or imagine) precisely as much as may be useful in the interest of the human herd, the species; and even what is here called usefulness is in the end only a belief, something imagined and perhaps precisely that most fatal piece of stupidity by which we shall one day perish."

Farley folds the papers from which he had just read and puts them in his side jacket pocket. He looks over the class for any signs of life. There are five or six still alive, which is more than enough. "Let's talk about this passage," he says, aiming his words at the living, "not by trying to understand it or analyze it, but by asking perhaps a few new questions relative to it about thinking and the problem of human consciousness. Did the passage inspire any of you to formulate a new question?"

Kyle Billingsly, a boy near the back who has said nothing all semester, is first to raise a hand. "Yeah, what I wonder is how consciousness can ever be conscious of itself...I mean it seems a consciousness can only see things or be conscious of things outside itself, so it could never really be conscious of itself. I mean it's like a kitten running in circles trying to catch its own tail, if you see what I mean."

Farley is amazed and says, "Great question, Kyle. You've been doing your homework. Today we won't answer the questions, we'll just ask as many as we can. Who's next?"

"I'd like to know what you read, so I can read it again, Mr. Farley. But I was wondering if it is possible to think without words. I mean, is our thinking limited to our language system? You read a parenthesis that said something like language is the metaphysics of the people. I see this to mean that we break down the world with the language we have. Put us in a different culture with a different language and would reality look different?" David looks to Elizabeth for a reaction as he stops.

"Good," Farley says.

Before class is over, the following questions are also asked (some are spoken, some remain quiet in the consciousness of the thinker):

Didn't people like Einstein and Newton have consciousnesses that knew the truth?

Do dogs and cats and elephants have consciousnesses, too? If so, what's the real difference between theirs and ours?

How can I get Elizabeth's consciousness to think I'm the sexiest son-of-a-bitch on the planet?

Has Mr. Farley ever been in an insane asylum?

Is the American consciousness—with all the TV-media-hype

shit—exactly what was being talked about as far as the herd stuff goes?

What is consciousness anyway?

Why does Mr. Farley make life so complicated?

Is the world that presents itself in my consciousness really superficial and surface? Is language, is all talk, a falsification and corruption of reality? Is there such a thing as reality?

Is there a chance Mr. Farley will let us out early so we can beat the lines in the cafeteria?

If I could get Elizabeth out of my consciousness, would I take all this shit more seriously?

Was human consciousness really different back in the Stone Age? Has it really collectively changed? Will it change in the future?

What does Mr. Farley's wife look like?

How am I going to pass this course?

If I can't turn consciousness—my consciousness—on and off, then doesn't it in a sense rule me? What is the difference between me and my consciousness? Is my sense of myself a function of the herd he was talking about? Where do I begin and the herd ends?

Has she ever been laid? Who says I don't have an organ that knows something?

⁓

HI FARLEY,

If I didn't know any better, I'd say I'm falling in love. I know what I said in my last epistle, but this time it's different: the object of my desire is myself. Wasn't it Oscar Wilde who said to love oneself is the beginning of a lifelong romance? For the first time since gold was discovered in creamy California, I like myself. Now when I undress in the crooked depths of our bathroom, I don't examine my flesh for blemishes. I don't even look at the mirror. I just walk into the shower. Is this a sign of hope? When I encounter Aphrodite in the supermarket I no longer sense hell scuttle through my heart at the thought of her crinkled in your arms. In the past, every beauty I saw wreaked instant havoc. Is it because you're eight hundred miles away? I doubt it. Before, if you were on the moon, I'd lose it while watching some Lolita prance on TV. O brain! Why didn't God make it waterproof? Anyway, I feel good. Maybe I'll finally get a lollipop.

I'm thinking maybe I should come and see your mother. You're second, though the idea of your perfumed underarms doesn't work against you. If you stamp it with your approval, I thought I'd drive the kids out as soon as school finishes. I assume her disease is not going to cure her, i.e. I'd better get there before it's too late. Plus I'd like to have another look at that Utah desert I used to hate while you were orgasming over its beauty behind the steering wheel. Maybe I'll find *something* out there after all. Part of my new diet, I guess.

You'll be proud to hear that Ricky's pulling nothing but A's in mathematics. He says numbers are more fun than letters. Throw that into your next lecture. Rosanne's world turns around stuffed animals, still. She's named that elephant you gave her for Christmas *Farley*. She says the nose is what did it.

Give your mother whatever regards make sense to her. If you want me to direct the Volvo toward that red desert, just say yes.

Clearly,
Carole

126

DEAR CAROLE,

Mother's typewriter is now mine. Our visit with Dr. Nichols went as expected and feared: Mother has been placed in the 24-hour care of the Hearts and Hands Nursing Home, recommended highly by the doctor himself and the doctor's grandmother. He asked her a few questions like "How have you been feeling?" and "Have you enjoyed your son's visit?" Her answers wove together strands of Carl's children, cousin Claris's boy, her husband's love of steak and lobster, the Milton boy playing with her son Larry, and the laundry that we should do before we drive to Dr. Nichols'. He checked her heart and blood pressure, left her in another room, and gently told me that she had slipped into another realm of being. He said that some people in her condition can first try a simple old folks home where they are more or less responsible for themselves and don't have constant surveillance. But he thought that given her rapid deterioration, she'd only survive such an abode for a month at most. So he suggested we skip the halfway house (my term, not his) and deliver her directly to the good people at Hearts and Hands. Am I relieved? Is life ever a relief? Only in so far as they are better equipped than I to change her diapers and provide her with medication. Our last few days together she lost either the desire to use a toilet or the notion of when to go. She also showed signs of not being happy, as if her mind was putting so many demands on itself that she never knew where to start. Doc called it depression. Great word. Rhymes with Cartesian. Which rhymes with simplification which rhymes with everything man does when he tries to understand what the hell is going on. All particulars get socked into the general. Anyway they say she needs drugs to keep her from going off the deeeeeep enddddddddd. Wonderful how there's always someone who knows what's good for us. I see her mornings and evenings and have been getting in 18 holes in between. The weather lately has been that deep blue sky with the air in the low 100s. The locals won't play in the afternoons, at least until somebody invents an air-conditioned golf cart. I, as you know, am a the-hotter-the-better sort of guy. So I joyfully putter from putt to putt in divine solitary. Then I beer in the clubhouse, bathe in the condo pool and sup in mother's spacious kitchen. The course is so empty I've even snuck Freda on a couple times. She removes the notion of number from the game: can't keep score when she's got the ball in her mouth. Anything she can see she retrieves. Anything she can sniff she pulls out of the rough.

As for your new love—there must be equilibrium in the universe: mother depresses as wife delights. Is the woman I'm writing the one I'll see when you get here?

Yours,
L.F.

THERE ARE DAYS when the world feels funny. The feeling might not begin with waking, but may come as you hunt your car keys to take a letter to the post office. You find them and you get in your car thinking maybe you shouldn't be going where you're going. Generally you spend your time doing things and speaking sentences that fit the plan that is your life. And then suddenly there is a day or part of a day when what you do does not seem right, does not seem to be what should be happening. You ignite the car and it lunges a bit and the connections between your foot and the gas pedal and your hand and the steering wheel are not clean, but seem loose and tentative. The ordinary inosculation that ties you to thing is amiss. Your extremities are sandpapered. When you cross other drivers their humanness appears suspect. They are neither ghosts nor incarnadine robots, nor are they man. They and their cars do not drive; they float like cirri or cumuli across a bay window. Where they are going is not a place or an end. When you park your car near the post office and begin to walk, your fellow pedestrians are in slow motion. Their limbs look not to be part of a whole, rather each moves to the beat of its own sermon. As you remove the letter from your pocket, you wonder if it is really yours. It could have been written by another and you despond as the girl behind the counter weighs it, stamps it, and tosses it into the tray marked Out of Town. You leave the post office and stand outside the door. The head that you feel balancing atop your shoulders turns not right nor left; you feel a slight burning in the eyes that see where the head points them and they are seeing a kaleidoscopic flock of bulbous automobiles that release and recall a sputter of somnambular knots. You find yourself back in your automobile which feels smaller than the last time you were in it. You think you are going to play golf but you think again and your thinking tells you you ought not to because something strange might happen and if it does you don't want to be on the golf course. You think the strange happening might be your mother's death because you remember that the day your father died you were supposed to drive to Tahoe to a seminar but you got as far as Sacramento and turned back and when you opened the door to your house in Moraga your wife handed you the telephone in a panic and it was your mother trying to tell you through frozen sobs that your father was dead. You know you have had days when you've sensed the same strangeness and nothing eventful has happened, but you think again of how you stopped at The Nut Tree for coffee and when you got back on the freeway you thought something was tugging you to avoid a weekend with Heidegger's apostles, so before Sacramento you made a U.

So you leave the parking lot and you drive to the Hearts and Hands Nursing Home even though you left there only an hour before. You walk past the receptionist on the grey-blue carpet through the corridor to Room 23. You knock softly and enter and find an aide changing your mother's underpants and your mother is saying there's no need to do so, there's no need to do so. You do not notice the aide has left and you take your mother's hand, but it moves away and begins fidgeting with the channel selector of the TV that you had not noticed was on. The hand gives it to your hand and your mother asks you, dear, could you help find Lucy. You know Lucy is not on because you watched it with your mother two hours before. You hear your mother ask you what time Larry will be back and you say you are Larry and you are back and you see irritation, you think. Then you ask how lunch was and you hear your mother say Carl joined her with his son and they went to the Burger King, and you don't tell her Carl has yet to get on a plane. You stay another ten minutes until the drugs the aide delivered drop your mother toward her nap. But before you leave she says and you hear, "I don't like living like this." You kiss her near the eye and you lower the air-conditioner a notch. You open and close the door timorously and you walk down the grey-blue carpet that seems softer than when you came.

You drive your automobile north to Snow Canyon and you find yourself walking in the pink fluxion of the sand dune. Above you red is part of the mountain like the red of the clay court you played tennis on when you had your honeymoon in Europe. Dirty white is the other part, but you don't look up long because you look down for snakes that are not there. You look horizontally and you see the dog walking because it is too hot to run and she squats to pee. You feel the clout of the sun feeling for the depths of your skin and you want a beer or is it the beer that wants you?

There are days that feel funny. On this one your mother does not die, and neither does anyone else you know.

THERE ARE SO MANY shopping centers on Highway 19 from Clearwater to New Port Richey that the speed limit, though marked 55, is more like 30. What can push man to build such ugliness if it isn't money? But the inhabitants of the area, like the alligators in the dying lakes, are oblivious to the antiseptic wasteland. They want the things being sold in the shops that are there to be wanted by them. And the wanting is not constant; it grows faster than the population and faster than the growth of the shopping centers. The consciousnesses of the people who come to buy on Highway 19 do not focus on the ugliness of the shopping centers because they see past the colossal monstrosities to the things they wish to buy.

Carl Farley had moved to Palm Harbor, Florida to make money. He was a part of the people who had put up the commercial bastions on Highway 19. At first he had made bundles. The money chain had been beefy. But the chain shrank and though the people around Highway 19 still wanted the things in the shops, they didn't have the means to buy them. The builders, of which Carl Farley was one, were biting the bullet, or—as it were—biting the edges of their chips.

Carl was in bed, awake, when his brother called. With business bad, the bed was a thorny cushion.

"I've tried to call you twenty times in the last month," Farley said, not unkindly.

"Sorry," Carl said, meaning it because it was his brother talking. "I've been down in Fort Myers trying to get a few things moving. It hasn't been easy lately."

"It hasn't been easy for mother either, Carl. When was the last time you talked to her?"

"I'd say about three months ago."

"Well, call her now and see what a glorious difference spring can make," Farley said, thinking it was something his wife would say.

"What do you mean?"

"I mean that we had to put her in a home which means that the doctor means it's hopeless which means that you won't know what she means when you talk to her."

"Is it that bad?"

"Just call her if you want a free sample. You've heard, I presume, of what the shamans call Alzheimer's? Well, she's not only a member of the club, but one of its fastest falling stars."

"Sorry," he said, meaning it because he was referring to his mother. "Where are you calling from?"

"I'm in her condominium. I've been here for a couple months. She's been in the Happy Hearts Club for a week now."

"What?"

"A nursing home, better known as Hearts and Hands."

"Is she in danger, Farley?"

"Do you know anyone who isn't? I only called to tell you that our mother is at the point of not knowing her sons. Do what you want with it. Mothers who don't know their sons take on a new form of life. I thought you might not want to miss the metamorphosis."

"I'll do what I can. Can I call her at the home?"

"You got a pen? It's the same area code. Six seven three, twenty-nine ninety-five. She's in Room 23. She should be there now. They usually don't give her her sleeping pills until about eight-thirty."

"Okay, I'll call. Thanks for calling. How's the sabbatical going?"

"If I cared enough to have a handicap, it'd be in the teens by now. And business?"

"Like I said, it's a rough period."

"Well, I suggest you call."

"I will."

"All right. See you, Carl."

"Guh-bye."

The god that Carl prayed to that night had much in common with the things for sale in the shopping centers on Highway 19. First, He was a noun. Second, His reason for being was to somehow make life easier or better. Third, He was desired. Fourth, He could be bought, not with cash only, but with acts of devotion and prayer. Fifth, He was not a verb; like a button-down shirt He could not be conjugated: there is no shirt, shirted, shirted and there's no God, Godded, Godded or maybe an irregular God, Gewd, Gewd. Sixth, He was, in the mind of the seeker, ever-changing. And seventh, He slipped in and slipped out, slipped in and slipped out of the consciousness of he who had truck with Him.

Carl decided to pray before calling his mother. As earnestly as possible he asked for her recovery and good fortune. When he finished, he decided it would be better to call her the next day.

IF I READ my calendar correctly, we have two more class periods before your exams begin. I thought we'd take the time to let you ask any questions that have been sticking with you, and we'll do our best to peek inside them and see what's on the other side. Metaphysics has been our subject. Metaphysics has been our object. Thinking has been our tool. Language our scalpel. The store stays open for another hundred minutes. Any customers?" Farley walks to his favorite spot near the window and leans his elbow on the wall. Then he says, "And please don't hold back—we're among friends. No question is idiotic. There are no judges among us."

A brief silence is broken:

"Mr. Farley, what's the difference between physics and metaphysics?"

"None that I can see, except maybe for the fact that historically metaphysicians rarely take their case to a laboratory or a nuclear playpen. They're both trying to get at what is."

"Aren't we all?"

"Good question. Are we? Does we include dogs and cats and mice and aardvarks and mosquitos and Californians? Teacher gives up."

"The day you read us the passage about consciousness, I thought to myself...(hesitation)...ah, the hell with it...thought to myself, all I really care about is how to weasle my way into the consciousness of this girl I love and make her think I'm the finest S.O.B. on campus. Is there anything wrong with that?" (pause until laughter dies).

"Not that I can see. Who's to say what thinking and consciousness are really all about? What do you think?"

"Well, I didn't try to think this while you were reading, but I couldn't stop the ol' consciousness from yearnin' and churnin'. I mean, are we animals or not?"

"Why is *yearnin' and churnin'* to be associated with animalistic behavior? As far as I know, no human has learned to speak tiger-talk well enough to understand the depths of tiger-consciousness."

"Mr. Farley, I have a friend taking the same class but with another teacher and they've spent the semester reading philosophers like Plato and Aristotle and Spinoza and then talking about what they read. Why haven't we done that?"

"Don't ask me, ask my horoscope. Maybe your friend's teacher wants to keep his or her job longer than I do. Really, I'd suggest you read Plato and Aristotle and Spinoza and ask yourself which makes you think more about metaphysics. I remember when I was eighteen or nineteen, reading Plato meant as much to me as a menu in a Russian restaurant. Teachers teach—I hope—in the manner they think gets the best results. What I'm trying to achieve is to get you to get beyond your normal mode of thinking, to get you to think about things in new ways."

"What's wrong with the old ways?"

"Another good question. I can only say that some of us might not be satisfied with the old ways, so we look for new ones. Metaphysics is supposed to be an effort to get at the real. If you don't think your way of thinking is getting there, you may attempt to plow fresh ground. Obviously, most people go through life more or less accepting what the world has handed them. There can be surface changes and variations in preferences and such, but the fundamental structures of how they perceive the world rarely are questioned. Now you can ask why try to get at the real? Why look in any new pockets? What guarantee is there that there is anything behind the surface? Why not watch TV all day? Why not accept what tradition has passed on? Is man capable of anything else? These are all things to think about and I've approached these questions the way I think is best."

"Mr. Farley, are most of the people in nut houses people who are obsessed with such questions?"

"I don't think so. There are plenty of people who live on Main Street and at the same time are digging new holes. I think the people in the nut houses—as you put it—are there for other reasons. There's no necessary connection between thinking and insanity as far as I can see. Remember, causality is a thick shell to crack."

"We haven't talked much about science this semester. Isn't scientific research the best way to find out what is true or real?"

"Science has eyes and ears and hands on its side. It makes things edible, palpable, understandable. But does this make the things true? Just because we can see and feel does not mean our seeing and feeling are, in fact, real. Real, maybe, to he who sees and has been taught that seeing sees reality. But does it?"

"What about religion?"

"Religion has a couple things on its side. First, death. If death as we know it did not exist, do you think religions would have the hold they do on people? I don't. Second, religion makes great use of our faulty vision of the causality we spoke of a minute ago. You have a sick child; you pray to God to cure him; he gets better; you say he got better *because* of God. Such thinking gives religion a highly seductive power. In fact it gives a lot of things a highly seductive power."

"Mr. Farley, I've enjoyed your class a lot, but I wonder if I've really learned anything."

"Glad you've had fun. I surely hope you haven't learned any-THING this year. If you have I'm a bad teacher. I'm not trying to teach you THINGS—I'm trying to teach you how to think about all those wonderful THINGS you learn in your other classes. Are those THINGS really THINGS after all? Is there such a THING as A or B? How does our thinking affect THINGNESS? Is thinking—or consciousness —A THING? Is there A THING that thinks? These are the kinds of cookies we're trying to munch in this class. What you've said is the supreme compliment."

"At the beginning of class today you said something about language being our scalpel. What did you mean?"

"We've only got a couple minutes left so why don't we save your question for the last lesson. By the way, in case any of you are wondering what your final exam is going to be like: you're going to be asked to write a question that interests you and then answer it. Nothing could be more difficult, right? See you next week for the last roundup."

THE MAROON WAGON pulled into a sixty-minute parking space next to the curb in front of the county building on 3ʳᵈ Street, downtown Las Vegas.

"Are we gonna eat now, Mommy?" Ricky said.

"We'll eat after we get a motel," Carole said.

"Is this where our motel is?"

"This is just the end of the pilgrimage."

"What's that?" Rosanne asked. "I thought we were gowin to the motel."

"It's the place where Mommy and Daddy gave each other a big kiss and said I do and then went to work on making Ricky and Rosanne. I just wanted to see it again before we go see Daddy."

"Why did you say I do?" Ricky asked.

"Cause that's what you say when you get married."

"You got married here in the parking place?"

"We got married in that building across the street there."

"I thought people got married in a church, Mommy."

"Daddy didn't want to. He thought this would be more romantic."

"That's dumb."

"He also didn't want anybody else to be there."

"That's dumb too. Didn't he have any friends or anybody?"

"Yeah, but you know Daddy likes to play golf by himself and get married by himself, I guess."

"Oh well, can we go to our motel now?"

"Sure."

It was seven, but the casino lights were already on as they drove down the Strip to the white motel across from the Aladdin. Farley had crossed the street at midnight and left Carole in bed with more pain than he knew and a kidney infection. He went in with thirty dollars and came home drunk at three with a hundred. He had thrown the money on the bed and said, "Baby, we're gettin' married tomorrow." And they did. Carole couldn't remember which room it had been and it looked like the place had new owners. She took a room near the pool. How in heaven does one decide to get married? she thought as she threw the suitcases on the bed. One doesn't, she answered. One rolls into it, like everything else.

The next morning she let the kids go swimming, then they drove up Interstate 15 through the lunar landscape toward St. George. He's right, she thought while the kids drew pictures of houses and flowers and suns in the back seat. Beauty was beckoning.

The two-hour drive took three and a half. The first emergency stop was to let Ricky vomit breakfast. The coke and pancakes were fighting for space in his little stomach. Carole pulled off the highway into the parking area of a Navajo jewelry stand. Ricky dry heaved, started to sweat, then burped and within seconds said he felt fine. But he needed water so they stopped at a gas station that had slot machines. Each child pulled the handle four times as Carole watched two dollars worth of quarters spin cherries, plums, oranges, lemons, and stars to fruitless halts. The last stop was at a resting spot just inside the northwest tip of Arizona. The children peed and threw water at each other as they washed their unsullied hands. They took off their T-shirts, climbed in the back and drew on each others arms and chest as they wended the last twenty miles between them and Daddy.

Daddy wasn't there when the Volvo pulled into Grandma's driveway. He was sitting on a chunk of lava-looking stone in the

belly of Snow Canyon watching Freda, watching rock, watching
the flamingo-colored sand, watching the vapid vapory sky,
watching lizards flee Freda, watching the baby aspens near and
round the campground twitter their pale green-silver leaves,
watching his mother seven miles away hunch and fold her arms,
her head flagging in gravity's grip, as she tells him, "Dear, why
don't you have lunch with Carl if you can take time off from school
today," watching his thinking as it wanders and wonders what
man, if any, has ever looked heavenward and earthward and inward and thought and felt (who cares for how long?) that there is,
has been, and always will be absolutely nothing behind what is
seen, that there is absolutely no meaning innate in anything anywhere, that the eye and heart flit and samba here and there until
eye and heart they are no longer without ever really knowing
anything or anyone, that all the thought of another world, another realm, a higher world, an inner world, even a lower world
that has wedged its way so ably into man's thinking is most likely
absolute and total falsity? Who, Farley wondered, has ever really
dived from a high solid rock into the ocean and held his head
under water long enough to see that in the deep of the deep there
are no good or bad fish, no higher or lower realms of being, no
real and unreal, no right or wrong, no yesterday or tomorrow, no
up or down, no in or out, no yes or no, no lines or circles or tri-
angles, no numbers 1, 2, and 3, no gods giving tickets to
otherworldliness, no sinners to sin, no choosers to choose, no
thinkers to think, no winners to win, no losers to lose, no knowers
to know, and no night, no day? Who has ever kept his head long
enough in the water such that when he emerges and walks again
on land, he sees man as that strangeness that attributes every-

thing to life except what it is? Has anyone, he wonders, looked into all the churches and laboratories and books and discourses and poets and thinkers and said, "I have neither heard nor read nor seen anything that has anything to do with what life actually is?"

Farley sat on lava-looking stone and wondered to a stop, while Freda sniffed—bin to bin—the trash in the corners of the campground.

I<small>T WAS</small> 110 in the shade and after two when Farley got back to Bloomington. The Volvo was in his mother's driveway, but the house was empty. He took off his shirt, grabbed a towel, left Freda inside, and walked to the condo pool. His wife, wearing dark glasses and a red and green flowered bikini he'd never seen before, was on her stomach in a flattened chaise longue. Rosanne was floating upright near the eight-foot sign, thanks to inflated plastic buoys around each bicep. In a thin puddle on the steamy asphalt between his mother and the hand rail leading into the shallow end lay Ricky. Unnoticed, Farley climbed over the low redwood fence behind the diving board, flipped off his tennis shoes, and intended to do a flying cannonball in the middle of the pool. He sprinted to the edge of the water but when he planted his left leg and pushed off, he felt a pop in his hamstring. His flying cannonball became a sprawled leaden flop.

"Shit," he said lugging himself to the steps below the hand rail.

"What happened, Daddy?" Ricky shouted, running to greet and save the floundering fish.

"I did something to my leg, guys, but it's nothing a couple of kids can't cure. Come and give your ol' Poppi a kiss."

"Poppi, Poppi!" Rosanne cried, as she motored with flailing arms towards her father.

"It's good to see you guys," Farley said and he wrapped an arm round each child. "Where's that camouflaged mother of yours? She get eaten by a shark?"

"She's lyin' down over there," Ricky responded, pointing a finger over his shoulder.

"Lemme get a glimpse of the world's eighth wonder." Farley kissed left and right on the two foreheads, then rose laboriously and limped out of the water like an aged penguin.

"Nice *entrée en scene*," Carole said, eyeing her husband of eight years plus through her Polaroid shades.

"To splash or not to splash, wasn't that the riddle? So how was the trip?"

"We saw where you and Mommy said I do," Ricky said.

"You what?"

"We drove up through Las Vegas," Carole clarified. "For old times sake, I guess."

"Any winners down there these days?"

"We played the machines, Daddy, but the cherries and yemons and stuff were mixed up so nothing came out." Rosanne had followed her father out of the pool. She grabbed a handful of fingers from his left hand. "Mommy gave us each some money."

"Now that's what I call a nice Mommy," Farley said. "Did you guys stay in a motel with a swimming pool?"

"Yeah, and I can swim across the pool under water sideways. Watch Poppi." Ricky dove in at the five-foot mark and struggled to the other side. His flagellate arms did twice the work of his legs, but chaos conquered and his proud head rose to meet air at the other side. "Se-hee, see Poppi," he said grabbing for land while his free hand slapped drippings from his face.

Before Farley could compliment his son, Rosanne screamed, "I can swim too, Daddy! Take off my floaties and I can show you! Take 'em off Daddy and go in the wadder and I'll swim to you." Daddy obliged and hobbled back down the steps into the pool. He stood about ten feet from the rail with open arms. "An ice cream cone says you can't make it to Poppi without stopping," he challenged.

"What about meee?" Ricky shouted.

"You too, but let Rosanne go first."

Farley watched his daughter, five years old and counting, stroll to the first step and focus her glazed wheaten eyes on his outstretched arms. Her puffy thighs, tanned twin stumps supporting a yellow polka-dotted torso, made ready for takeoff. "Are you ready?" he said. She threw back her hands and shuffled her feet.

"Wait, wait!" she said. "You're too far, Daddy!"

"Okay, but just a little." Farley shortened the width of the ocean by a foot and Lindbergh's historic voyage was duplicated in water.

"Me now, Daddy! Me!" Ricky cried.

"All right, but you have to swim across the pool. Then it'll be Mommy's turn."

"Across the pool! Come on! Rosanne only had to go ten feet!"

"Ice cream doesn't grow on trees, kid," Farley said. "And I hear you're old enough to be Zorro's brother."

Ricky swaggered round the pool to the deep end. His strut was his mother's; the oval butt and thin-but-meaty hips made his bathing suit look like a floating balloon. Life's luscious chain, Farley thought. Ricky stood over the water in pre-adolescent splendor, dove, paddled and battled to earn every lick of his reward.

"Good job, Ricky. We all knew you had it in you. You've won yourself a two-scoop trophy. Now let's think of a way to get Mommy's hair wet. You kids might not know this, but I fell in love with Mommy the first time I saw her with wet hair. It was love at first dip."

"Daddy, you're nuts. How can you fall in love with wet hair?" Ricky had recovered his breath.

"Just wait, kids. You can fall in love with things that aren't even there. But let's make Mommy earn her ice cream, then we'll head for the bliss of Baskin and Robbins. I propose that Mommy do the cannonball that I didn't do. What do you say guys?"

"Yeah!" came the high howl.

Carole slipped off her shades and rose from the chaise longue. "Farley dear, I used to think you were a teenager. Now I know I overestimated. But you are a cute toddler." It was that mellifluous telephone voice talking, the voice that filtered up from the depths of separation. "Bomb's away," she said and climbed swankily onto the diving board. Then with the grace of mating swans, she and the water colluded for a cool coitus interruptus.

"Yayyy Mommy!" the high howl screeched. "I never saw you do that before!" Ricky shouted when she surfaced.

"That was better dan Daddy's," Rosanne added.

"Thanks, kids. Sometimes it takes time to display all your talents." Carole climbed out of the pool. Farley limped toward her and they rubbed noses for the first time in heaven knows how long.

"How's your mother?" Carole asked when their heads fell apart.

"We'll go see her later. Let's get the ice cream first. I usually go about four," Farley said. He dragged himself to a shaded chair and began kneading the flesh on his injured thigh.

꒜

MASSIVE OBJECT Is Discovered
In Unusual Galaxy

Associated Press

NEW YORK—Astronomers have found a mysterious object about 100 billion times as massive as the sun, and they said it is either the largest black hole ever found or an unexplained phenomenon.

"The huge mass and its great concentration and darkness are puzzling and unlike any found previously," said Joss Bland-Hawthorn of Rice University, one of the discoverers. The object's mass is roughly equal to that of all the stars in the Milky Way galaxy, he said. Yet it is compressed into a space 10,000 times smaller.

The object was discovered by Mr. Bland-Hawthorn, Andrew Wilson of the University of Maryland, and R. Brent Tully of the University of Hawaii using the 88-inch telescope atop the extinct volcano Mauna Kea in Hawaii. They reported their findings in the April issue of the *Astrophysical Journal*.

They were searching for an unusual galaxy that emits a high level of infrared radiation called NGC 6240 when they discovered the object inside it. They were surprised to discover that the galaxy contains not one spinning disk, as most spiral galaxies do, but two. The first disk is similar to the spinning disk at the core of most visible spiral galaxies. But the second disk was quite different.

By measuring the speed of rotation of objects around the disk, they concluded that its mass was at least 40 billion times that of the sun and possibly as much 200 billion times the mass of the sun.

This Farley read in a stray *Salt Lake Tribune* as he sat in a school-like desk in Baskin Robbins while he, children and wife licked and bit a single almond fudge, a double bubble gum and Swiss chocolate, a double peanut butter and strawberry swirl, and a single raspberry sherbet. Everyone went with the sugar cone.

He thought the article not unusual.

GRAMMA! GRAMMA!" Ricky shouted, running through the door of Room 23 and pouncing on his grandmother's bed. "We brought you a present. Give it to her, Rosanne, before it melts all over the place." Rosanne handed Adell Farley a small carton of peppermint ice cream and a white plastic spoon.

"Oh, my goodness, what a surprise," she said, working her body to a sitting position.

"Eat it, Gramma, before it's a milkshake."

"Oh well, we'll have to have dinner first, then we can put it in the fridge."

"You don't have to have dinner first, Gramma. You can just eat it now," Rosanne said helpfully.

"Well, this is a surprise. I'd better get ready to go to the doctor's, and then we can have dinner. Have you seen the telephone book? I can't seem to find it."

"No, Gramma, I don't know where it is, but I can help you find it if you want." Ricky's eyes roamed the room to no avail. "But eat your ice cream, then we can look for it."

Farley and Carole stood outside the open door. Farley had told the children to go in first and give their grandmother the treat. "Your ears are newly arable," Carole whispered. She reached up with her closest hand and flicked a finger at a small grove of hirsute stalks shooting up from his earthy left lobe.

"Guess the mirror's been too far away to notice," he whispered back.

"So's your mother, no doubt."

"The kids are adorable."

"Do you think she knows who they are?"

"Partly."

"Which part?"

"That I wouldn't know."

"Shall we go in?" was their final whisper.

"Mom," Farley said, "Here's another little surprise."

Carole rounded the bed and kissed her mother-in-law on the soft pouch of skin below the cheekbone. She set a box of See's candies on the night table.

"Well, this is a surprise. The children and I were just getting ready to go to the doctor's. And then there's the ice cream that we were trying to find with the telephone book here just a minute ago," she said and looked for a spot to set down the ice cream. She put it on the candy box.

"Gramma, you better hurry and eat or else you're gonna make a big mess," Rosanne advised.

"How are you, Adell?" Carole finally said. "It is good to see you."

"Oh yes, you are. I was just going to get dressed and find the telephone book and the children here are helping me. My cousin Claris will be moving in soon so I need to call her to arrange a few things. Larry is teaching...tomorrow, so I want to call for now. Yesterday she was here so she'll be back before the doctor." She looked at Ricky and Rosanne and added, "They'll be able to play together I'm sure."

"Yes," Carole agreed. "Would you like the ice cream?"

"It would be fine after, so I think we should be getting ready."

"Okay, everybody," Farley declared. "Why don't you kids quickly gulp down the ice cream and then we'll all take Grandma out for a ride in that beautiful Volvo covered wagon. Snow Canyon is waiting for us and so is Freda. How about that?"

Farley cumbersomely lowered himself into the metal frame chair near the television and watched his children share the errant snack with a minimum of warfare. They must have sensed, he thought, that Grandma's room wasn't their standard eristic playground. Discord needs a propitious environment. Then he saw Carole help raise his mother from her bed and without conversing, proceed to dress her as one would garb a patient before wheeling him or her in for major heart surgery. When a moment feels like it might be a last—like an airport goodbye—human hands get delicate.

When the kids finished the ice cream, they scrambled up onto Farley's lap. Ricky put his lips to a hairy ear and asked most quietly if there was anything wrong with Grandma. "Nothing that a couple kids can't cure," a whisper answered.

M OSES LOOKS THROUGH the windshield into the day. The covered wagon climbs out of St. George toward Winchester Hills, a new residential development that is slow to move. For twelve thousand you can buy an acre lot and for another fifty you can throw on a four-bedroom house. Moses would put palm trees in front of his. Would the neighbors think them out of place? Would the snakes? He looks over the land that he has not looked over since he looked over it that morning after leaving his mother who is now beside him looking over the land too, he thinks. Moses looks right to see the land that the wagon is passing. He sees the land then sees his mother who is not looking over the land but who is looking at the dashboard and/or the glove compartment and/or somewhere that he is sure he cannot see. Her eyes and bent head remind him of Freda's when a storm is near and swelling and she—Freda—scrambles to his side, points her nose to the ground, and waits; and while waiting the eyes freeze, then wander, then supplicate, revealing more than usual the red blood vessels set in the white membrane around the black and walnut brown circles of the pupil and iris.

Moses' eyes flip back to the road that is rapid-firing stripe by stripe the broken white line under what looks to be the left front wheel but isn't. Moses is in his lane.

Then the eyes rise and the motion stops. Falco peregrinus, *oiseau de jour.* But this time the hawk, as it looks on the day from the purring fence, does not pray. It wings left, following the sign for Snow Canyon and begins the descendent glide. Its seeing sees the erstwhile mother that quietly comes from the bathroom into its darkened space with a cool folded washcloth in one hand and a bottle of rubbing alcohol in the other. She lays the bottle on the headboard that holds the plug-in/portable radio that in the pre-sleep night oozes the divine jabber of the Oakland Oaks games until the Oaks and the league fold. Before the folding, the radio brings the Word: "Kenny Sears-with-a-turn-around-from-the-corner—Got-it!"..."That's twenty-six for Sears!"..."Oaks-forty-eight-Pipers-forty-three!"

The words in muffled treble traverse the dark and God lives. Then the league calls it quits and God dies but is resurrected: "Rogers-down-the-middle-behind-his-back-to-Thurmond—HOLY-TOLEDO!"..."Hightower-to-Mechery-from-the-corner-GOOOOD!" ..."Warriors-eighty-nine-Pistons-seventy-two!"

The radio is off when she sets the bottle on the headboard. She eases onto the bed hip-to-hip and fixes the washcloth on the feverous forehead. Then one hand uncaps the bottle, the other hand pours the charged liquid into the cupped first hand and the rubbing begins on the legs and feet. Moses sees Moses purr to the euphony of the rubbing. Were the radio on speaking the words *Sears* or *Hightower*, all the grace of God would fill the night and flow through the spongy nest.

Moses looks anew over the land that is the canyon that rises as the wagon drops: on the right, rising white furls like vertical waves; on the left, the lava stuff like coal spilt from a huge train. He wants to urinate and watch the thin yellow stream steam on the baking rock.

"Can you turn up the air-conditioning a little?" Carole says from the back seat. "We can't feel anything back here."

"Are you too cool, Mom?" Farley asks as they wind down to the bottom of the canyon.

"I'm fine, Larry," she says.

"Let me know if it's too much."

"Yes, if it is, it will be fine, I think, or will we be late? Do we need to be going to meet Claris?"

"Can we get out and play in that pink sand?" Rosanne wants to know on seeing the dune.

"Not today, guys. It's too hot out there for Grandma. We'll come back some time in the morning. This ride's for Grandma. But when we get back to the house you can go swimming again if you want before bed."

"Bed!" Ricky interrupts. "It's not even dinner time yet."

"Then you can go swimming before dinner. Across the pool is worth a cheeseburger—unless Mommy wants to rustle up some elephant safari stew," Farley says.

"Eyiphants! You can't eat Eyiphants!" Rosanne shouts.

Carole leans forward and whispers an "I didn't think you cared" in the chauffeur's left ear.

Care, the chauffeur thinks, is the dividing line between life and death.

"It's getting a bit chilly," his mother says.

"I'll turn it down," he says.

FARLEY ROLLED off his wife with a tender grunt and onto the side of his mother's bed where he'd been sleeping since she had moved into Hearts and Hands. He had chosen to vacate the guest room because he knew she'd never be back and because the master bedroom had a southerly view. Mornings he could draw the curtain, lift the shade, and get an eyeful of a usually empty sky cut at the bottom by a vast encampment of sagebrush and old dry earth.

"Do you love me?" Carole asked in more than a whisper.

"Did the African King?"

"Forget history, Farley. Let's stick with the eternal present." She propped up her head and said, "Well...?"

"My father taught me never to talk about anything serious after the sun goes down or three beers—whichever comes first."

"Since when is love a serious subject for you?"

"Forget the love part. It's the *you* part that scares me." Two Farley fingers strolled across Carole's belly. She took it as a sign that only one barrel of the shotgun had fired, but her hand to his crotch brought nary a throb.

"In case you never noticed, my goal in life has been to be loved."

"To be or to feel?"

"Both, I guess."

"My inkling is that the latter happens, but the former doesn't hold up well under a microscope."

"You're so damned romantic, Farley."

"It is after nine, but didn't you nicely say that your self now feels love for itself? And wasn't the implicit nitty-gritty that this is what matters?" Farley said, thinking it wasn't unpleasant to have somebody to talk to.

154

"I'd say it's Act One of a two-act play."

"How many actors in the ol' play?" he asked.

"Does it make any difference? Two at a time seems to be all that's necessary."

"Didn't you also say that you had had this juicy revelation that you had never really loved anybody?"

"That's why I'm asking. Now I think I'm ready. I'm thirty-four, the world turns, and I'd say I've spent enough time in the Dark Ages. So do you or don't you?" Carole let her elbow slide and dropped onto her back.

"If I said I did, I'd be lying and if I said I didn't, I'd be lying too. There ain't no truth where there ain't no truth. But it's good to see you." The ring of the phone rescued the shipwrecked.

"Don't answer it," Carole said.

"It might be my mother's home." Farley lumbered from the bed toward the kitchen on a leg and a foot. It felt like he'd pulled the muscle a little more climbing to and from the serendipitous sockets in his wife. Freda, who had taken to sleeping under the Japanese night table next to the bed, followed Farley out of the room.

Carole reached down and grabbed the nightgown she'd taken off half an hour before. I should have known better, she thought, than to have imagined a Viking could metamorphose into a Romeo. She sat up, slipped the nightgown over her girlish shoulders, and looked round the foreign room. The carpet, thick and twine-like, was salmon pink and the walls were a light powdery green shaded toward turquoise. Mrs. Farley had adorned them with two bamboo-framed Japanese prints, one over the bed and the other next to the door leading to the bathroom: trees, leaves, bridges, mountains and men, inky flips of an oriental wrist. Carole stood and took a few steps to the walk-in closet. Her husband's suitcase and clothes lay in a heap on the floor. What her mother-in-law had left behind was arranged seasonally on the right rack. First the summer blouses and cotton dresses, then the sweaters and polyester suits, finally the wool apparel and the winter coats. The left rack, presumably once Farley's father's, was empty except for wood, plastic and metal hangers and two aged, sexless raincoats. Carole had an urge to rake away dead leaves. She went to the bathroom, brushed her teeth, turned off the light and got back into bed.

"Who was it?" she asked when Farley rejoined her.

"It was Carl. He's coming next week."

"When?"

"Friday night. I said I'd pick him up in Las Vegas."

"When did he last see your mother?"

"At least two years ago. The alligators have been nibbling at his checkbook."

"Does he know everything?"

"As much as you can push through a telephone."

"So where were we?" Carole asked stacking two pillows which Farley took to mean she wasn't ready to sleep.

"Somewhere after nine o'clock."

"You were trying to spare yourself a lie as I recall."

"Was I? Look, Carole," Farley said as a shot of pain jolted his leg, "let's just say I'm probably a bad investment—for you anyway. You want the heavy breathing, the panting, the poetry, the declarations, the lies. It's not me. I lost the golden touch somewhere in the shuffle."

"Who's to say they're lies?"

"Nobody's to say—everybody's to believe what they will. I

don't really mean lies. I mean grunts. I don't grunt the way you want me to grunt. Love grunts remind me of TV grunts which remind me of congregational grunts. All fine for the grunters and gruntees, but I just don't see the circus that way. Sorry."

Carole flipped on the light behind her head and sat half up. "What do you believe in, Farley? Tell me just once."

"Nothing anybody else I know believes in."

"What is that supposed to mean? Don't you believe your mother's lost it?"

"Lost *it*. No. Lost what? Lost the right way to order lunch in a restaurant? Lost what time it is? What day it is? Who's coming for dinner? Who says any of this is anything to lose? She might no longer know Tom's telephone number or Dick's last name or Harry's summer itinerary, but who decreed that these things need to be known in the first place?" Farley rubbed the back of his wounded thigh. His wife stared at the quilt bedspread and ran a tight hand under her nightgown. Farley swam on. Daddy's curfew had already been violated. "There never was an *it*. My mother's relation to the world has never been a constant. Ditto for everybody. A cloud isn't an *it*. It's a big whirl and everybody knows it but no one wants to admit it. My mother's world now is a new whirl, a different whirl, a less common whirl, but *it* she hasn't lost. *It* was never there in the first place."

"You're ice, Farley. You've walked too far. The calluses are too thick."

"Whence came the value of slobber?"

"I didn't say slobber."

"Didn't you? What did you say then?"

"Your mother has Alzheimer's disease and you're spinning

clouds. Where's your heart? Where's your feeling for your mother?"

"See Carole, I don't grunt the way you want me to. As far as I can tell, slobber, heart, and feeling are perfect synonyms. You want redemption. You want a world that's not there. Fine. I don't blame you. But I don't see it that way. I want my mother the way she is. Now. Right now. There's no going back to the full-blooming flower driving her sons to Little League, then to the ice cream store for a postgame treat, then the tucking of little Farley in bed with a kiss on a silky forehead. To want it back—this would be the crime against my mother. To love what she was and cry because it's not there for yourself anymore—is that what you want to call having a heart? I'd say that's love turned on its head. And to cry because the past isn't there for her is to totally miss nature's message: the shit ain't constant.

"Love it or leave it, hey Farley?" Carole said, not far from tears.

"Not a bad way of putting it."

"I think I'm tired," she said. "It's been a long day." She poked out the light and curled up like a dormant fox.

Before sleep, Farley's hand found her crotch. Here there was life. Like I said, he thought when the donut split in two: the shit ain't constant.

CARL WAS TO arrive the following day and Farley felt he needed some air. He said goodbye to his family at the breakfast table where the kids had an angled view of the cartoon parade on Grandma's swivel-based TV. They slurped colored balls of airy oats and ingested sounds and images that had inherited little from the ducks and mice and bears of Farley's youth. Ricky and Rosanne's heroes wore metallic hexagonal masks, toted laser swords, sprayed lightning bolts, and cruised through space at meteoric speeds in flattened vehicles shaped like a flock of migrating birds. They were capable of walking and talking, but other than that they failed to resemble any human beings Farley knew. They never ate, never slept, never joked, and never paddled hopelessly after a member of the opposite sex. As far as he could tell, their existences revolved around destruction. Good and evil seemed imprinted in their universe. The fence had but two sides. Farley sensed a Christian influence.

He put his golf bag in the trunk of the Toyota and Freda in the back seat, but he wasn't sure where he was going to go. He drove to the center of St. George and stopped at the large drugstore on the hill at the east end of St. George Boulevard. Since his parents had moved to the town, the store had changed names and owners at least three times. Business, like rain, he thought, was rarely a sure thing in the desert. He rubbed the cyst on his left bicep then got out of the car. Since he had started teaching, a gang of the apparently harmless fatty balls had grown round his abdomen. Only the lonely cyst on his arm had him worried. Hadn't a baseball player for the Giants had cancer in his pitching wing? And wasn't the stuff as omnipresent as weeds? Getting through life without a cancer was like walking through a shopping mall without buying anything. He rubbed the arm again, then stepped on the rubber mat that swung open the door to Osco's.

At nine-thirty in the morning, the aisles—though wide enough for passage of a mid-sized car—were empty. Farley looked in amazement at what people bought. If they didn't buy the stuff, it wouldn't be in there. He wandered to the men's toiletries. There were fifteen kinds of dressing for the hair on his head. The only one that wasn't packaged was in a transparent heart-shaped bottle and called *Tres Flores*. It looked like what Clark Gable must have used. Farley unscrewed the apple-green cap and took a whiff. He poured a few drops into the palm of his hand and worked it into his scalp. Tres Flores had a new patron. After paying the cashier the asking price, he went back to the car and rubbed a few drops between Freda's ears and along her nape. He decided then to drive to Zion's Canyon, but not until he had had a cup of coffee and read the newspaper. For this he chose the Sugarmill Restaurant over Denny's, primarily because at the Sugarmill the walls and waitresses were baby blue.

Big Bang Theory
Has Fizzled Out

LAWRENCEVILLE, New Jersey—A sweeping revolution in science's view of the universe is taking place, a revolution like that of Copernicus, Galileo and Kepler. The Big Bang theory is crumbling, as Ptolemy's earth-centered cosmos did then.

For 20 years a growing band of scientists led by Hannes Alfven, who won the Nobel Prize in physics in 1970, has argued that the Big Bang never happened—that the observational evidence is consistent with a universe that has existed forever,

always changing and evolving—a universe without beginning
or end.

   With the new observations of huge structures in the universe,
a debate has begun in earnest. The pessimistic chaos of the Big
Bang, doomed to inevitably decay or to end in a Big Crunch,
may be replaced with a universe evolving from a past without
beginning to an unlimited future.

Three cheers for the home team, Farley said to himself, thinking
the cold cereal companies could make a bundle by calling their
next invention *The Big Crunch* or *The Big Bang*. Then he thinks if the
outside is timeless and infinite, odds are the inside is as well.

   "Another spot of coffee, hon?" the waitress asked, holding the
half-filled pot near her waist like a gun.

   "I think that'll do me," Farley said with a pinch of the Utah ac-
cent. He then watched the woman, who—with one motion of
perfect fluency—pulled a pencil from behind her ear, grabbed a small
paper pad from her apron pocket, scribbled what looked to be two
figure eights, tore off the top sheet, laid it on the counter and slipped
the corner under a glass ashtray. Farley saw Heidegger's Dasein at
work: you drive a car for hours without feeling the steering wheel;
you wash the dishes and can never remember actually touching
any object; you play eighteen holes of golf without ever really
being conscious of hands to club. Dasein as being-in-the-world.
Dasein as being-in-the-Sugarmill-coffee-shop. Dasein as plucking-
three-silver-to-the-eye-quarters-from-the-pocket-of-the-pine-
green-shorts-and-placing-them-on-the-counter-and-rising-and-
thanking-and-rubbing-the-cyst-and-feeling-being-towards-death.

   Three cheers for the home team, meaning Being, Farley thought
when he regained the car and Freda in the Osco parking lot. He
didn't know if he wanted to vomit or sing hallelujah. He drove to
Zion's with an eye on the road and another on the rest.

———

AFTER RETURNING to the United States from Paris, David Jorgensen spent his time painting houses in the day and reading books after dark. He painted to earn enough money to eat; he read books like *The Magic Mountain*, *The Trial*, *The Brothers Karamazov*, and *Fear and Trembling* to have somebody to talk to. At least that's what he told himself. That morning in Paris, when he had vowed to throw off the cloud of pessimism, was still real for him. The headaches were gone but the subject of his existence continued to haunt him—at least to haunt him in such a way that he spent his free time reading the aforementioned works instead of drinking beer, watching Monday Night Football, and chasing pussy in bars. He did this for a year until the smell of paint had him hallucinating. He couldn't concentrate on a book in the evening and by day he found he would paint the same corner of a shutter or a window sill for what seemed to be hours. He once fell off his ladder as he was doing a rain gutter.

He had been living in Livermore with his parents who only charged him for board. When he complained of his hallucinations, his father suggested he go to work for the government. Doing what? David had said. Whatever governments do, his father had responded. He was given an interview in San Francisco and was asked if he had his choice would he prefer chasing the nation's most wanted criminals or painting benches in national parks. He quickly thought that there couldn't be enough benches to bring on the hallucinations, so he opted for the latter. Though the question had been hypothetical, David had taken it seriously and was not surprised when he was shipped to the southern Utah desert and Zion

National Park. He left home tearfully and happily and to his relief was assigned to collect the entrance fees at the west end of the park.

When Farley pulled up in the Toyota with a five-dollar bill in hand, there was the earless left side of David's head under the wide brimmed ranger's hat.

"David Jorgensen," Farley said, poking his nose through the open window.

"Mr....Mr. Farley!" David exclaimed. "What are you doing here?"

"Now what kind of question is that from my best ex-student? I'd say I'm baking like the rest of us."

"It is hot out there."

"How good it is to see you, David," Farley offered sincerely. "How long have you been here?"

"About six months. I can't believe it's you." He looked up and noticed two bulbous recreational vehicles behind Farley's car. "Are you staying here for a while?" he asked, hoping Farley would understand his intention.

"Listen, I know you've got work to do, and I've got to get my dog to a toilet, but if you're free today for lunch I'd like you to be my guest."

"Great. I'm off from one to two." A horn blasted from one of the campers. Farley had an inkling to jump from the car, point a full-blown index, and bellow "CAN'T YOU SEE THE FUCKING KID'S ONLY GOT ONE EAR!" knowing that pity was an emotion most idiots shared. But he didn't. "We could meet at the restaurant in the lodge inside the park," David said hurriedly.

"Fine. See you at one."

"Oh, you've got to keep your dog on a leash, Mr. Farley."

"Okay," he said.

Farley parked in a half-shaded spot at the lodge. With two hours before the luncheon date, there was time for euphoria, an orgasm of his mind in the wide open beauty of the national park. He opened the trunk, unzipped the side pocket of his golf bag, and filled the pockets of his shorts with beat up balls. His hiking stick a five-iron, he and Freda began trekking up a northbound trail. A sign advised them that the whole loop would be eight miles. They'd have to settle for an hour up and an hour back.

The first two hundred yards were lined with white ash and aspen that had been planted circa 1919 when the government turned the place into a park to keep its citizens' filthy paws off the jewelry. After that the path narrowed, shade disappeared, and most visitors headed back to their cars. For half an hour, Farley and Freda climbed alone. The rock—the color of Farley's sunburnt forearms—was cut in sloping layers. Above them it was muddy white like the north walls of Snow Canyon. Come, come ye orgasm, he thought as he gazed at the beauty of the rusty twinkle. Nothing doing—his mind was a blank, his heart dull. Was it the heat? He took off his golf shirt and wiped the sweat-balls that were worming down his flank. Freda was unleashed, Farley thinking liberty might mysteriously have a cooling effect on both of them. He sat on a smooth porous boulder and stared at the grove of monoliths on the other side of the canyon. Science would say it was all a couple hundred million years old. But we desert mice know better than to thumbtack beginnings, middles, and ends to stony waves. We know better than to make stone of our wavy little thoughts. And we borers of black holes know better than to pop our heads into the light and split earth from sky from cloud from tree from me.

Come ye orgasm, come. Why won't it come? wondered Farley. How the hell can the jewel get any twinklier than Zion's Canyon?

They climbed higher to a thin plateau. The ground was something between dirt and sand. One by one Farley dropped the golf balls.

He loosened his back with a half dozen practice swings. Then, while he fidgeted over his first shot, Freda snatched the ball-to-be-hit with a single snap of the jaw. She shook her hips and rolled her head to announce the beginning of *You Can't Catch Me*. The rules, Farley knew by heart :

1. Freda slides her front paws forward and lowers her head between them;
2. She keeps her haunches high, her tail pointing upward and wagging like a metronome;
3. Her eyes, like live marbles, glare at Farley;
4. She is all heat and happiness, then...;
5. When Farley moves, Freda moves;
6. The moment is all Freda's.

Freda watched Farley conk the other balls to the canyon floor, then followed him back down to the car. She was happy. She heard Farley say casually, "Sometimes it's there and sometimes it's not." For her it meant water, but for Farley it meant something else.

$\mathcal{P}$

WELL WHAT A SURPRISE I am here I am here   there it was when I we were talking then yesterday with Larry   she was here yes and they gave me the ice cream I thought

hold on while I look because we have to put it in the fridge after she was dressed for the doctor but I'm sure I saw it there under where did we go then after that when it was   cold over there maybe near the TV   I think then they will play fine together with   then   I'll see if she's here

yes last time   it was on the table with the telephone can you then I'll tell you   so we went to the Sizzler with Carl this time because the doctor had it before you called

oh yes the children

hold on while I go there where she is here

I think she went with Larry to the store where we found it but I thought okay then I have to get dressed and

while I just get her so then you can call

Who's this a male voice asked.

It's her son Larry Farley   Farley said.

I was just in here cleanin'   the voice said and she kept givin' meee the phooone

It's okay, I just wanted to see if my wife had been by to see her

Not that I know of, but if I seee her I'll tell her yooou called

Farley wondered how this vowel-stretching Texan had ended up in St. George, Utah

Just tell her I'll stop by in the late afternoon

Will dooo, Mr. Farley She's doin' juzzz fine

Thanks Tell her I said goodbye

He hung up hearing the coins jingle to the pit of the machine and pushed his way out of the phone booth Freda leapt to greet him but was neck-yanked to the ground thanks to her leash and a fence post

Hang on a minute Farley said I'll see if I can rustle up a bowl of water from the lodge   She sat with ears pointed and her eyes followed his form as he climbed three wooden stairs and disappeared

Mr. Farley David said

I'll be right there I've just got to find a bowl and some water for my dog Why don't you get us a table in the meantime

Where'd you find that golf club

It found me I think Be right back

Seeing him come down the three steps the dog leapt once then remembered the neck-yank and sat with impatient paws and moist eyes   drank the water from the styrofoam bowl Farley watched the pink tongue slap and catch the water til the bowl looked newly manufactured then he put them both in the car cranking down the windows half way   Forget the fucking thieves Maybe Freda'd bite off the arm before it got the trunk latch and the golf clubs Maybe she'd lick it and beg pets

So how'd you end up here Farley said

Well it's a long story like all stories I guess David said but after coming back from Paris I painted houses for a year or so then my Dad suggested I apply for a government job and this is where the goose laid me

Nice lay Farley said remembering Elizabeth and feeling a tight tie to the man on the other side of the checkered red tablecloth and what maybe his life had been

I could have done worse You know I didn't even know this canyon existed until they sent me   Are you just vacationing

I took a year off Farley said   then gulped the ice water the waitress set down with a How 'er you fellas today   And it turns out my mother lives in St. George and is not doing so well   water   so I've been with her for the past couple months

David said sorry to hear it then Farley said You were in Paris you say

Do you remember the girl next to me in your class Elizabeth well I guess you could say she broke my heart though now that I look back   I've got lots of time to think out here it was more like   ah   more like my heart was a ripe strawberry and I threw it in the first milkshake that walked by

I'd say Farley said you chose pretty well   She was a helluva nice girl

Yeah I know Anyway the next year I took off to Paris with another girl to try to   ah what   to try to lay a BandAid on the wound   water   and in a sense I guess it worked

How did you like Paris Farley asked

I'd say I liked the perspective it gave me The whole trip did I remember how you used to talk about perspective and how even the bright lights of academia seemed to lack it

Miss could we get a little more water

Do they serve beer here David

No I'm afraid not

How long did you stay

Six months all told   water   I slowly began to realize that me and my little California culture were looking at the world with blinders on

Farley said Your mind had a pretty good start back then in class
    So what'll it be today fellas
    I'll have a cheeseburger and an ice tea
    Lemme have the Reuben sandwich and I'll have an ice tea too
    Cole slaw or french fries with your sandwiches boys
    Cole slaw
    Twice

Nice Farley thinks thinking of nothing but the cole slaw his mother used to make with raisins and walnuts in it Then he opened the cellophane around a toothpick   thinking mother   life has taken you here   Where will death take you   then thinking blather   Life doesn't give and take nor does death because we are both   We are not their doings   We are them Then saying David you know you were probably the best student I ever had to the boy's sublime delight   I just used to hope that your brain wouldn't get the best of you   What I mean is I think there are people bright enough to see that the tunnel can look pretty grim but there are few who are bright enough to see themselves on through out the other end into the light

You said that once in class David said

Did I   It's amazing what I can't remember saying Farley said thinking that everybody's an Alzheimer's case insofar as nobody remembers everything and maybe nobody really remembers anything   We just think we do   tucked like we are in our collective convenience cocoons

Then he thinks of Tillich saying something like the thinker loves both the truth he discovers and himself for discovering it and has to admit that he gives himself pleasure in his thinking about his mother's case   that is his sentimental unsentimental acceptance of

169

what is   zzzzzzzz   a black fly on the water glass
So are you going to teach next year David asks
Unless you have a better idea Do you plan on going back to school
Doubt it
You would have made a fine teacher
I just didn't want to do what you do for fear of not living my own life
Good choice
Here's those sandwiches fellas   If I can get you anything else just give me a holler.

WALKING DOWN THE corridor in the B Building toward Room 424, Farley recalls what he had been thinking prior to and on awakening that morning. He calls it thinking rather than dreaming, but he knows no difference between the two. He remembers: he is moving through a large unending tube; the tube is not plastic or metal, but is made of the people and objects in his world; he is skimming through it unable to stop at any fixed point; *he* is his consciousness; there is no braking it, no controlling it; it flies and nowhere and on nothing can he bring it to a clean halt.

Now the thinking of the early morning is the thinking of his walk through the corridor. The mind will not be stopped. And to think I call it *my* mind, he thinks.

He pulls the door and enters Room 424. There is a small bouquet of white handpicked daisies in a paper cup on his desk. He lifts the flowers and smells very little, but enough. He is touched and he removes his oft-worn corduroy jacket. Life, he thinks not knowing why, is a vacation from death. Then he thinks life, death, and vacation have nothing to do with each other or are maybe one and the same.

"Thank you and good morning," he says as he rubs his shoulder to the windowed wall. "Well, this is it. The last hour of the last day of the Going-Out-Of-Business Sale. But don't buy anything hastily. Remember how much crap goes out the door at sale time. Does anybody remember what we're peddling today?" Farley walks to his desk and sits on it cross-legged—a meditative pose.

"It was language," David says without raising his hand.

"Language," Farley agrees. "Now some of you might wonder why we're talking about language on the last day of *An Introduction* to *Metaphysics* class. Well, we could have talked about it on the first day or we could have thrown it in the middle somewhere, but I wouldn't be doing my job if I didn't slip it in at one point or another. In fact, I think every teacher in the school should talk about it in every class offered. But they don't. Why? I hope by the end of the period you'll ask yourself the same question." Max Lippett has raised half an arm.

"Mr. Farley, I have a friend taking a *Philosophy of Language* class this semester and he says that in four months he hasn't made any sense out of anything. How are we supposed to get anywhere in forty-five minutes?"

"What would we do without you, Max?" Farley says. "I can only say that you are not your friend and I'm not your friend's teacher. And who's to say that time—weeks, months, years—is necessary to get your gorgeous unshaven minds to work on something. I know philosophers who say more in one sentence than others say in entire books. Maybe four months on a subject deadens the brain. Maybe forty-five minutes is too much. You decide, Max. I'm just going to try to peck a couple holes in the tree to let in a little light."

"Gotcha coach," Max mumbles to those around him.

"Let's begin with a little story about my son Ricky," Farley offers as he walks back to the window near Elizabeth's chair. "A couple months ago Ricky came home with a new word...fuck. (Pleasure bumps go through most of the students.) He walked around the house saying *fuck, fuck, fuck* until the word started coming out more *foke, foke, foke*. Being the diluted psychologist I am, I didn't say anything to him until I heard the *foke* come out. Then I asked him if he knew what a *foke* was in the French language—by the way, the

French spell it p-h-o-q-u-e. He asked me what the French language was and I told him it's a different set of words and sounds that people in other parts of the world use instead of English. Then I told him that *FOKE* in French was an animal, a seal. He said the kids in school didn't say it meant a seal. I told him I knew they didn't, but that if he ever went to France and said *Foke you* the people would think he was saying something about a cute amphibious creature. 'But Daddy,' Ricky said, 'A foke isn't really a seal. A seal's a seal, right?' (David laughs out loud.)"

"So...what's the moral of the story?" Farley asks.

(Don't "phoque around" with the French, Max Lippett thinks but doesn't say. Then, just before Christine Lasenger thinks Mr. Farley is dirty on top of it all, Max thinks he'd phoque Elizabeth all the way to the Arctic Circle. David's hand goes up and Max tunes back in.)

"David."

"I guess we all think our language is the real language or at least the right one."

"Keep going. What do you mean?" Farley says with a smile.

"I think I mean that for your son—and for most people—the word seal means something that is supposed to be real—that is, we think our language corresponds to reality, if you see what I mean. I guess I mean we tend to think our language is somehow sacred, that it tells the truth when it describes the world. Maybe I'm not being too clear."

"Maybe the sea's not very clear here, David," Farley says. "But I'd say what you're getting at should make everybody think a little. Who can add to what David has said? Let's forget the *foking phoque* now." (More pleasure bumps in most of the wayfarers.)

"I remember in a class about the American Indian," Elizabeth offers hesitantly, "that the Indians have different verb tenses than we do and that their language is quite different from ours."

"I don't know much about the Indians," Farley says, "but I think we can assume that different languages are going to express different ideas about life and the world. Now David used the word sacred. I think he chose a good word. Let me ask you to think about where language came from. Who invented language? God? Man? Some idiot who couldn't get a fire started? A genius who saw being for exactly what it is? We have twenty-six letters in our alphabet. Should we have more? Less? Is twenty-six the perfect combination? How about words: Is the dictionary sacred? Are there just enough words? Too many? Too few? What do you think?"

Arthur Windell throws his arm over the top of his head.

"Arthur."

"Now that I think about it, I think man made language and given that man makes a lot of mistakes, he probably did the same with words. He probably left out a whole lot and put in too many in a few places. I mean why do we have ten different words to say think: like ponder, reflect, imagine, reason, call to mind and all the rest?"

"Good example, Arthur. So you think languages might be defective? Let me ask you this: What are languages supposed to do?"

"Describe the real world, I think," David says.

"All right," Farley partly agrees. "Do they?"

David again raises his hand. "It seems that this semester the notions *real* and *world* have kind of gone through the meat grinder. Now *language* is going there too. It strikes me that it's a little tough to say anything about all three."

The kid can do it, Farley thinks, hoping the boy will survive the meat grinder. Then he says, "Now let's do this: let's take one word—any noun—and see if this word tells the truth, that is, let's see if the word describes something real. Or maybe the word is more real than the thing it's supposed to describe. But we better hurry. The shop closes in ten minutes. How about the word window?" Farley taps the glass with a knuckle. "Does the word window do what it's supposed to do?"

The class is silent. The teacher thumps the window again. "Might it not be," he says, "that a window is an infinity of atoms and electrons and crystals and what not? Don't we use one word to simplify our collective sense of communication, whatever that might be? Isn't communication maybe a social experience that has nothing to do with reality? Why communication at all? Maybe language tells us something about man and his society, but nothing about reality or the world as such." Farley pockets his hands and begins walking among the students. "If a window is made of atoms and atoms are always in motion—or are motion or energy or whatever—then maybe a window is not a noun at all, but is really a verb. Maybe nouns—all of them—are only the result of faulty human thinking or simplistic seeing. Because the window looks static we call it an *it*, a thing, a window. But would it be an *it* under a high-powered microscope?"

The teacher goes back to the front of the class and plops into his chair. He looks at Christine Lasenger whose eyes are hidden behind the fingers on her forehead. He wonders if he has said enough but says, "And what about this *I* that thinks? If there's a noun of nouns, it's the *I*. Is there an *I* that thinks, or is there only thinking? Do you remember our little experiment way back when,

when we tried NOT to think? Is the *I* really a subject—a noun, a fact, a thing—that thinks or acts, or might there be something else going on? Does the wind really blow? Or is there only blowing? But then maybe blowing is, too, a simplification. Maybe the blowing shouldn't or can't be separated from the tree that gets blown. Maybe in the end (what end? he thinks) language is only a collective device; it herds people together. But does it refer to anything real in the world? That is, anything real other than itself?"

Farley stops.

David loves him.

Max Lippett has heard the word blowing and is lost in his Elizabethan fantasy.

Christine Lasenger is lost, period. She wants out.

Arthur Windell remembers hearing that Farley has once been a basketball player. He thinks he'll invite him to the gym for a little one-on-one.

Elizabeth's thinking, without detail, goes from a one-on-one to a one-in-one to 1-in-o to 1-in-0.

Kyle Billingsly wishes Farley would go on, but can see he won't. The store is closed.

＊

THERE ARE DAYS when you think you'll find beauty but you don't. You will drive to and from a place like Zion Canyon—a place you have been to before and have found lovely—and your eyes and insides never tell you that what you are looking at is in any way glorious. You may feel hunger or absence or a dim irritation with man, road, rock, or yourself. You will think and remember when the place was beautiful, but you know that you and the place are never the same twice.

On such a day you leave the Canyon driving south then west through towns named Hurricane and Leeds and the houses, trees, sidewalks, and gas stations do not appear to have been sculpted by God's hand. Instead they obtrude and exude putrescence. Nature, you think, is cancerous. And you think that everything—absolutely everything—is nature and there is too much of it. Too much to die. Too much to come. Too many holes. Too much space.

And then as you and the car wend through the verdure along the Virgin River you know that what you see out there is a mirror of what is inside you. Or do you? you think. Might it not be the inverse: the inside mirroring the outside? Or might it not be there is no in nor out?

In any case you know that you are on your way to see your mother and you will be there in half an hour. And you know and remember that you can be made to feel what you are now feeling by the sight of the purple scabbed sores on your mother's arms and by the stale medicinal smell of her final home and by the nurses whose hands know dead bodies like yours know golf balls.

What you feel on such days at such times is not anger or

anguish or disgust, but is like what you feel when you see the favored photograph of yourself at age two on the wall in the bedroom of your mother's condominium. Then and there your deliciously fatty arms and soft cherubic cheeks are tied to undying eyes that stare at something that is not in the picture. You are wearing a seersucker jumper with a wide collar and your nose is like a button. You have been told that the picture is of you, for otherwise you would never know. Looking at it, you cannot make sense of the then and now; you cannot make sense of the slits in time and space. But you know that nature has no means or mechanism for making sense of itself so you sit or stand or walk or drive and feel what you are feeling until the feeling fades as it does now when you turn the steering wheel to catch Interstate 15 south. And with the road now straight as a pencil you flip on the radio that is tuned to a country western station and while the songs of dented hearts whine for your attention, you smile and throw your right hand in the back seat and feel for your dog's head. The head finds your cupped hand and the fingers rub the white diamond between the ears and then the ears themselves are each stroked thrice to their tips. Then you two-hand the wheel anew and drive past the green-fresh golf course on Washington that you have yet to play. Then you feel your foot release the accelerator and you and the car drift right onto the St. George Boulevard exit ramp. You lope through a string of green lights between the garden of motels whose red orange pink blue and white neons will not come on for another two hours. You glance right at the drugstore you were in that morning before you knew where you would go. This time the cyst on your left arm does not get rubbed and you make one left turn and a right and you run into the sign for Hearts and Hands.

There are days when you know you will not see your mother forever. You know that your foot falling on the mat that opens the sliding door to her home will one day have no reason to be there. The door opens and you are greeted by the stale medicinal smell that bathes you until you have been in it long enough to no longer notice it is there. You walk and then hear the gentle knock that is your knuckle on the partly open door of Room 23 and you enter to find your mother sunken in the soft chair behind the thin portable table that holds her dinner that is partially on her plate, partially on the floor, and partially on her blouse and lap. The purple curved vein near her nearest ear is the target of your kiss that falls after you have said "Good to see you Mom" and she "Larry," the same "Larry" that you have heard for as long as you can remember. What follows is the same set of sounds you have heard for as long as you can remember except the order in which they are spoken resembles nothing out of the past:

> You came when I   that we were doing I think
> if Lettie said I don't think we should   then I
> want to this is not here if we do
>
> Do you want me to take your tray away Mom
>
> I thought we could see the children first and we
> the potatoes there   right then because didn't they
> want it
>
> The food always looks pretty good It is isn't it They
> seem to make an effort
>
> She came then when the Milton boy was a doctor   the

dishes flower were her first that if you have   we
think to there   when Lettie it I just thought with
both of it so it will do do they

Has Carl called Mom

Oh yes he wanted it   so we can with the Sizzler I think
it could we have them too she wanted to say before then

Would you like some more water

No   no   I don't think that's a good time because if you
I think then Lettie the boys   better because they then do

I went to Zion's Park   It's always a nice place to see

Do they have one there if you want the   with a small portion
to the   they do usually

Your mother looks tired but before you ask her if she'd like to
lie down the phone rings and it is your brother saying something
came up and he won't make the plane tomorrow but he'll come as
soon as he can. You put the phone in its place and when you ask
your mother if she would like to lie down she says yes so you push
back the table and as you help her stand you are careful not to put
a finger on the purple sores and you escort her the two steps to her
bed. She sits and you lay her down and sideways and lift her legs
and bend them in such a way that they face the wall with her head.
You see her eyes slowly close and you rise and pull the curtains
then you return to the bed and sit with your right hip near her
head. You watch your right hand lay itself on her silver-blue hair
while the fingers feel for scalp and you watch them curl and uncurl

and gently dig. You see her eyelids cringe but you doubt it is pain; you imagine they are working toward sleep. You watch her and now feel the fingers of both your hands rub the heat that is her head and you see the body and at the same time you feel the tears in you swell and pop and drip. They come warm and fine; you know you won't be talking together any more that day.

There are days when you stay on a bed with a head in your hands like an opal until you feel it sleeps. Then you rise and softly set it centered on a thin yellow-cased pillow. On your way to the car you meet no one until the door opens and you sit. Then a dog paws you from behind and leaps licking for your waggish wet face.

JON FERGUSON lives in Lausanne, Switzerland, where he teaches high school English and coaches the Lausanne pro-basketball team. He is the author of two books published in French, *The Best of Schmaltzy* and *Neitzsche for Breakfast*.